THE
Rainbow Fairy
❧ Book ❧

EDITED BY

Andrew Lang

SELECTED AND ILLUSTRATED BY

Michael Hague

Books of Wonder
William Morrow and Company
NEW YORK

Printed in the United States of America.

1 3 5 7 9 10 8 6 4 2

Library of Congress Cataloging-in-Publication Data
The Rainbow fairy book / [compiled] by Andrew Lang ; illustrated by Michael Hague.
    p.   cm.—(Books of wonder)
    Summary: A collection of more than thirty fairy tales for young readers of all ages.
    ISBN 0-688-10878-4
    1. Fairy tales.   2. Tales.   [1. Fairy tales.   2. Folklore.]   I. Lang, Andrew, 1844–
1912.   II. Hague, Michael, ill.   III. Series.
PZ8.R13   1993
[398.21]—dc20   92-33449   CIP   AC

Books of Wonder is a registered trademark of Ozma, Inc.

Watercolors were used for the full-color art. Pencil was used for the black-and-white art.
The text type is 13½ pt. Goudy Old Style. The display type is Goudy Thirty.
Book design by Marc Cheshire

Contents

Introduction

❦

IN THE WORLD of literature, few people have ever led so diverse
and accomplished a career as Andrew Lang. Author, poet, critic, scholar—
Lang was all these and more. But it was as the editor of his acclaimed "Colored
Fairy Books" that he achieved his greatest fame.

Born in the Scottish countryside in 1844, Lang was raised on the area's
numerous local legends and fairy stories, the collections of Charles Perrault,
Madame d'Aulnoy, and the Brothers Grimm, and the marvelous literary works
of Hans Andersen, Walter Scott, Charles Dickens, and Edgar Allan Poe.
Throughout his adult life he earned his living from his work as a writer, editor,
and influential critic, and as such was instrumental in encouraging and further-
ing the careers of such great writers as Robert Louis Stevenson, H. Rider
Haggard, J.M. Barrie, Rudyard Kipling, Sir Arthur Conan Doyle, and E. Nesbit.

Though Lang wrote several original books for children—including *The
Gold of Fairnilee* (1888), *Prince Prigio* (1889), and *Prince Ricardo of Pantouflia*
(1893)—none brought him great fame or success. But in 1899, a collection of
classic fairy stories edited by Lang was issued under the title *The Blue Fairy Book*
and became an instant success. The following year (1890) Lang assembled
another collection under the title *The Red Fairy Book*. This also was well
received. Over the next twenty years, Lang would edit ten more Colored Fairy
Books, bringing the series to a total of twelve volumes, encompassing tales and
legends from nearly every continent and culture around the world.

The popularity of *The Blue Fairy Book* was a great surprise to Lang's
publishers. At that time, the "realistic" stories about "everyday" children's lives

Introduction

by such authors as Juliana Horatia Ewing and Mrs. Molesworth were so popular as to dissuade most publishers from issuing any other kind of children's books. It was the common wisdom that children were no longer interested in fairy tales. Fortunately, Lang knew otherwise and proved it with his fairy books.

Though these collections were by far his most successful books, Lang was haunted for the rest of his life by the public's belief that he *created* these stories or that he did the retellings. In fact, he did neither and issued a disclaimer to this notion in the preface to nearly every one of the Books.

> A sense of literary honesty compels the Editor to keep repeating that he *is* the Editor, and not the author of the Fairy Tales. . . . The Editor's business is to hunt for collections of these stories. . . . These explanations have been frequently offered already; but, as far as ladies and children are concerned, to no purpose. They still ask the Editor how he can invent so many stories—more than Shakespeare, Dumas, and Charles Dickens could have invented in a century. And the Editor still avers, in Prefaces, that he did not invent one of the stories.
> —from *The Crimson Fairy Book* (1903)

> In truth I never did write [the fairy books]. . . . The fairy books have been almost wholly the work of Mrs. Lang, who has translated and adapted them from French, German, Portuguese, Italian, Spanish, Catalan, and other languages.
> Nobody really *wrote* most of the stories. People told them in all parts of the world long before Egyptian hieroglyphics of Cretan signs, or Cyprian syllabaries, or alphabets were invented. They are older than reading and writing, and arose like wildflowers before men had any education to quarrel over. The grannies told them to the grandchildren, and when the grandchildren became grannies they repeated the same old tales to the new generation.
> —from *The Lilac Fairy Book* (1910)

The stories in the collection you hold now in your hands were selected by Michael Hague, the artist. The Colored Fairy Books are some of his childhood favorites and choosing from among the more than 300 stories collected by Lang was not an easy task. Undoubtedly, there will be those who disagree with some of the choices, lamenting a personal favorite that was omitted, but the purpose of this collection is not to present the most popular of the stories Lang collected, but to introduce a new generation to the breadth and depth of the

Introduction

fairy tales in Lang's books—in short, the very best of Lang.

Toward this end, Michael Hague has selected not only the beloved, familiar tales from French, German, and English tradition and the literary work of Andersen, but also included stories of India, Spain, Lapland, Japan, Scandinavia, Rhodesia, and China. And he has used his illustrations to capture the magic and majesty of these timeless tales. By lavishly illustrating these stories with twenty-three full-page watercolors and nearly fifty pencil drawings, he has created windows into these fairy-tale worlds that reflect his own artistic vision. From the simple barnyard of the Three Little Pigs to the dense, germanic forest of Snowdrop to the dark cobblestoned streets of the Ratcatcher, his illustrations highlight each story's romance and mystery.

To close, I would like to address those who question the validity and importance of fairy tales in our modern world and those who worry that children might misunderstand their meaning or fail to distinguish fantasy from reality. Andrew Lang faced just such critics over 100 years ago when he wrote the following in his preface to *The Green Fairy Book* (1892):

> There are grown-up people now who say that the [fairy] stories are not good for children, because they are not true, because there are no witches, nor talking beasts, and because people are killed in them, specially wicked giants. But probably you who read the tales know very well how much is true and how much is only make-believe, and I never yet heard of a child who killed a very tall man merely because Jack killed the giants, or who was unkind to his stepmother, if he had one, because, in fairy tales, the stepmother is often disagreeable. If there are frightful monsters in fairy tales, they do not frighten you now, because that kind of monster is no longer going about the world, whatever he may have done long, long ago. . . . Therefore, I am not afraid that *you* will be afraid of the magicians and dragons; besides, you see that a really brave boy or girl was always their master, even in the height of their power.

What was true then is even more so today. It is through the exploration of these fabulous tales—told in one form or another all around the world—that we can discover those hopes and dreams that unite all people, regardless of geography or culture.

—Peter Glassman

Rapunzel

Once upon a time there lived a man and his wife who were very unhappy because they had no children. These good people had a little window at the back of their house, which looked into the most lovely garden, full of all manner of beautiful flowers and vegetables; but the garden was surrounded by a high wall, and no one dared to enter it, for it belonged to a witch of great power, who was feared by the whole world. One day the woman stood at the window overlooking the garden, and saw there a bed full of the finest rampion: the leaves looked so fresh and green that she longed to eat them. The desire grew day by day, and just because she knew she couldn't possibly get any, she pined away and became quite pale and wretched. Then her husband grew alarmed and said:

"What ails you, dear wife?"

"Oh," she answered, "if I don't get some rampion to eat out of the garden behind the house, I know I shall die."

The man, who loved her dearly, thought to himself, "Come! rather than let your wife die you shall fetch her some rampion, no matter the cost." So at dusk he climbed over the wall into the Witch's garden, and, hastily gathering a handful of rampion leaves, he returned with them to his wife. She made them into a salad, which tasted so good that her longing for the forbidden food was greater than ever. If she were to know any peace of mind, there was nothing for it but that her husband should climb over the garden wall again, and fetch her some more. So at dusk over he got, but when he reached the other side he drew back in terror, for there, standing before him, was the old Witch.

"How dare you," she said, with a wrathful glance, "climb into my garden and steal my rampion like a common thief? You shall suffer for your foolhardiness."

"Oh!" he implored, "pardon my presumption; necessity alone drove me to the deed. My wife saw your rampion from her window, and conceived such a desire for it that she would certainly have died if her wish had not been gratified." Then the Witch's anger was a little appeased, and she said:

"If it's as you say, you may take as much rampion away with you as you like, but on one condition only—that you give me the child your wife will shortly bring into the world. All shall go well with it, and I will look after it like a mother."

Rapunzel

The man in his terror agreed to everything she asked, and as soon as the child was born the Witch appeared, and having given it the name of Rapunzel, which is the same as rampion, she carried it off with her.

Rapunzel was the most beautiful child under the sun. When she was twelve years old the Witch shut her up in a tower, in the middle of a great wood, and the tower had neither stairs nor doors, only high up at the very top a small window. When the old Witch wanted to get in she stood underneath and called out:

> "*Rapunzel, Rapunzel,*
> *Let down your golden hair,*"

for Rapunzel had wonderful long hair, and it was as fine as spun gold. Whenever she heard the Witch's voice she unloosed her plaits, and let her hair fall down out of the window about twenty yards below, and the old Witch climbed up by it.

After they had lived like this for a few years, it happened one day that a prince was riding through the wood and passed by the tower. As he drew near it he heard someone singing so sweetly that he stood still spellbound, and listened. It was Rapunzel in her loneliness trying to while away the time by letting her sweet voice ring out into the wood. The Prince longed to see the owner of the voice, but he sought in vain for a door in the tower. He rode home, but he was so haunted by the song he had heard that he returned every day to the wood and listened. One day, when he was standing thus behind a tree, he saw the old Witch approach and heard her call out:

> "*Rapunzel, Rapunzel,*
> *Let down your golden hair.*"

Then Rapunzel let down her plaits, and the Witch climbed up by them.

"So that's the staircase, is it?" said the Prince. "Then I too will climb it and try my luck."

So on the following day, at dusk, he went to the foot of the tower and cried:

"Rapunzel, Rapunzel,
Let down your golden hair,"

and as soon as she had let it down the Prince climbed up.

At first Rapunzel was terribly frightened when a man came in, for she had never seen one before; but the Prince spoke to her so kindly, and told her at once that his heart had been so touched by her singing, that he felt he should know no peace of mind till he had seen her. Very soon Rapunzel forgot her fear, and when he asked her to marry him she consented at once. "For," she thought, "he is young and handsome, and I'll certainly be happier with him than with the old Witch." So she put her hand in his and said:

"Yes, I will gladly go with you, only how am I to get down out of the tower? Every time you come to see me you must bring a skein of silk with you, and I will make a ladder of them, and when it is finished I will climb down by it, and you will take me away on your horse."

They arranged that, till the ladder was ready, he was to come to her every evening, because the old woman was with her during the day. The old Witch, of course, knew nothing of what was going on, till one day Rapunzel, not thinking of what she was about, turned to the Witch and said:

"How is it, good mother, that you are so much harder to pull up than the young Prince? He is always with me in a moment."

"Oh! you wicked child," cried the Witch. "What is this I hear? I thought I had hidden you safely from the whole world, and in spite of it you have managed to deceive me."

In her wrath she seized Rapunzel's beautiful hair, wound it around and around her left hand, and then grasping a pair of scissors in her right, snip snap, off it came, and the beautiful plaits lay on the ground. And, worse than this, she was so hard-hearted that she took Rapunzel to a lonely desert place, and there left her to live in loneliness and misery.

But on the evening of the day in which she had driven poor Rapunzel away, the Witch fastened the plaits on to a hook in the window, and when the Prince came and called out:

> *"Rapunzel, Rapunzel,*
> *Let down your golden hair,"*

she let them down, and the Prince climbed up as usual, but instead of his beloved Rapunzel he found the old Witch, who fixed her evil glittering eyes on him, and cried mockingly:

"Ah, ah! you thought to find your lady love, but the pretty bird has flown and its song is dumb; the cat caught it, and will scratch out your eyes too. Rapunzel is lost to you forever—you will never see her more."

The Prince was beside himself with grief, and in his despair he jumped right down from the tower, and, though he escaped with his life, the thorns among which he fell pierced his eyes out. Then he wandered, blind and miserable, through the wood, eating nothing but roots and berries, and weeping and lamenting the loss of his lovely bride. So he wandered about for some years, as wretched and unhappy as he could well be, and at last he came to the desert place where Rapunzel was living. Of a sudden he heard a voice which seemed strangely familiar to him. He walked eagerly in the direction of the sound, and when he was quite close, Rapunzel recognized him and fell on his neck and wept. But two of her tears touched his eyes, and in a moment they became quite clear again, and he saw as well as he had ever done. Then he led her to his kingdom, where they were received and welcomed with great joy, and they lived happily ever after.

The Steadfast Tin Soldier

❦

THERE WERE ONCE UPON A TIME five-and-twenty tin soldiers—all brothers, as they were made out of the same old tin spoon. Their uniform was red and blue, and they shouldered their guns and looked straight in front of them. The first words that they heard in this world, when the lid of the box in which they lay was taken off, were: "Hurrah, tin soldiers!" This was exclaimed by a little boy, clapping his hands; they had been given to him because it was his birthday, and now he began setting them out on the table. Each soldier was exactly like the other in shape, except just one, who had been made last when the tin had run short; but there he stood as firmly on his one leg as the others did on two, and he is the one that became famous.

There were many other playthings on the table on which they were being set out, but the nicest of all was a pretty little castle made of cardboard, with windows through which you could see into the rooms. In front of the castle stood some little trees surrounding a tiny mirror which looked like a lake. Wax swans were floating about and reflecting themselves in it. That was all very pretty; but the most beautiful thing was a little lady, who stood in the open doorway. She was cut out of paper, but she had on a dress of the finest muslin, with a scarf of narrow blue ribbon around her shoulders, fastened in the middle with a glitter-

18

ing rose made of gold paper, which was as large as her head. The little lady was stretching out both her arms, for she was a Dancer, and was lifting up one leg so high in the air that the Tin Soldier couldn't find it anywhere, and thought that she, too, had only one leg.

"That's the wife for me!" he thought; "but she is so grand, and lives in a castle, whilst I have only a box with four-and-twenty others. This is no place for her! But I must make her acquaintance." Then he stretched himself out behind a snuffbox that lay on the table; from there he could watch the dainty little lady, who continued to stand on one leg without losing her balance.

When the night came all the other tin soldiers went into their box, and the people of the house went to bed. Then the toys began to play at visiting, dancing, and fighting. The tin soldiers rattled in their box, for they wanted to be out too, but they could not raise the lid. The nutcrackers played at leap-frog, and the slate-pencil ran about the slate; there was such a noise that the canary woke up and began to talk to them, in poetry too! The only two who did not stir from their places were the Tin Soldier and the little Dancer. She remained on tip-toe, with both arms outstretched; he stood steadfastly on his one leg, never moving his eyes from her face.

The clock struck twelve, and crack! off flew the lid of the snuffbox; but there was no snuff inside, only a little black imp—that was the beauty of it.

"Hullo, Tin Soldier!" said the imp. "Don't look at things that aren't intended for the likes of you!"

But the Tin Soldier took no notice, and seemed not to hear.

"Very well, wait till tomorrow," said the imp.

When it was morning, and the children had got up, the Tin Soldier was put in the window; and whether it was the wind or the little imp, I don't know, but all at once the window flew open and out fell the little Tin Soldier, head over heels, from the third-story window! That was a terrible fall, I can tell you! He landed on his head with his leg in the air, his gun being wedged between two paving-stones.

The nursery-maid and the little boy came down at once to look for him, but, though they were so near him that they almost trod on him, they did not notice him. If the Tin Soldier had only called out "Here I am!" they must have found him; but he did not think it fitting for him to cry out, because he had on his uniform.

Soon it began to drizzle; then the drops came faster, and there was a regular downpour. When it was over, two little street boys came along.

"Just look!" cried one. "Here is a tin soldier! He shall sail up and down in a boat!"

So they made a little boat out of newspaper, put the Tin Soldier in it, and made him sail up and down the gutter; both the boys ran along beside him, clapping their hands. What great waves there were in the gutter, and what a swift current! The paper boat tossed up and down, and in the middle of the stream it went so quick that the Tin Soldier trembled; but he remained steadfast, showed no emotion, looked straight in front of him, shouldering his gun. All at once the boat passed under a long tunnel that was as dark as his box had been.

"Where can I be coming now?" he wondered. "Oh, dear! This is the imp's fault! Ah, if only the little lady were sitting beside me in the boat, it might be twice as dark for all I should care!"

Suddenly there came along a great water-rat that lived in the tunnel. "Have you a passport?" asked the rat. "Out with your passport!"

But the Tin Soldier was silent, and grasped his gun more firmly.

The boat sped on, and the rat behind it. Ugh! how he showed his teeth, as he cried to the chips of wood and straw: "Hold him, hold him! he has not paid the toll! He has not shown his passport!"

But the current became swifter and stronger. The Tin Soldier could already see daylight where the tunnel ended; but in his ears there sounded a roaring enough to frighten any brave man. Only think! at the end of the tunnel the gutter discharged itself into a great canal; that would be just as dangerous for him as it would be for us to go down a waterfall.

Now he was so near to it that he could not hold on any longer. On went the boat, the poor Tin Soldier keeping himself as stiff as he could: no one should say of him afterward that he had flinched. The boat whirled three, four times around, and became filled to the brim with water: it began to sink! The Tin Soldier was standing up to his neck in water, and deeper and deeper sank the boat, and softer and softer grew the paper; now the water was over his head. He was thinking of the pretty little Dancer, whose face he should never see again, and there sounded in his ears, over and over again:

"Forward, forward, soldier bold!
Death's before thee, grim and cold!"

The paper came in two, and the soldier fell—but at that moment he was swallowed by a great fish.

Oh! how dark it was inside, even darker than in the tunnel, and it

was really very close quarters! But there the steadfast little Tin Soldier lay full length, shouldering his gun.

Up and down swam the fish, then he made the most dreadful contortions, and became suddenly quite still. Then it was as if a flash of lightning had passed through him; the daylight streamed in, and a voice exclaimed, "Why, here is the little Tin Soldier!" The fish had been caught, taken to market, sold, and brought into the kitchen, where the cook had cut it open with a great knife. She took up the soldier between her finger and thumb, and carried him into the room, where everyone wanted to see the hero who had been found inside a fish; but the Tin Soldier was not at all proud. They put him on the table, and—no, but what strange things do happen in this world!—the Tin Soldier was in the same room in which he had been before! He saw the same children, and the same toys on the table; and there was the same grand castle with the pretty little Dancer. She was still standing on one leg with the other high in the air; she too was steadfast. That touched the Tin Soldier, he was nearly going to shed tin-tears; but that would not have been fitting for a soldier. He looked at her, but she said nothing.

All at once one of the little boys took up the Tin Soldier, and threw him into the stove, giving no reasons; but doubtless the little black imp in the snuffbox was at the bottom of this too.

There the Tin Soldier lay, and felt a heat that was truly terrible; but whether he was suffering from actual fire, or from the ardor of his passion, he did not know. All his color had disappeared; whether this had happened on his travels or whether it was the result of trouble, who can say? He looked at the little lady, she looked at him, and he felt that he was melting; but he remained steadfast, with his gun at his shoulder. Suddenly a door opened, the draft caught up the little Dancer,

and off she flew like a sylph to the Tin Soldier in the stove, burst into flames—and that
was the end of her! Then the Tin Soldier melted
down into a little lump, and when next morning the
maid was taking out the ashes, she found him in the
shape of a heart. There was nothing left of the little
Dancer but her gilt rose, burned as black as a cinder.

24

Cinderella
or The Little Glass Slipper

ONCE THERE WAS a gentleman who married, for his second wife, the proudest and most haughty woman that was ever seen. She had, by a former husband, two daughters of her own humor, who were, indeed, exactly like her in all things. He had likewise, by another wife, a young daughter, but of unparalleled goodness and sweetness of temper, which she took from her mother, who was the best creature in the world.

No sooner were the ceremonies of the wedding over but the mother-in-law began to show herself in her true colors. She could not bear the good qualities of this pretty girl, and the less because they made her own daughters appear the more odious. She employed her in the meanest work of the house: she scoured the dishes, tables, etc., and rubbed madam's chamber, and those of misses, her daughters; she lay up in a sorry garret, upon a wretched straw bed, while her sisters lay in fine rooms, with floors all inlaid, upon beds of the very newest fashion, and where they had looking-glasses so large that they might see themselves at their full length from head to foot.

The poor girl bore all patiently, and dared not tell her father, who would have rattled her off; for his wife governed him entirely. When she had done her work, she used to go into the chimney-corner, and sit down among cinders and ashes, which made her commonly be called

Cinderella

Cinderwench; but the youngest, who was not so rude and uncivil as the eldest, called her Cinderella. However, Cinderella, notwithstanding her mean apparel, was a hundred times handsomer than her sisters, though they were always dressed very richly.

It happened that the King's son gave a ball, and invited all persons of fashion to it. Our young misses were also invited, for they cut a very grand figure among the quality. They were mightily delighted at this invitation, and wonderfully busy in choosing out such gowns, petticoats, and head-clothes as might become them. This was a new trouble to Cinderella; for it was she who ironed her sister's linen, and plaited their ruffles; they talked all day long of nothing but how they should be dressed.

"For my part," said the eldest, "I will wear my red velvet suit with French trimming."

"And I," said the youngest, "shall have my usual petticoat; but then, to make amends for that, I will put on my gold-flowered manteau, and my diamond stomacher, which is far from being the most ordinary one in the world."

They sent for the best tire-woman they could get to make up their headdresses and adjust their double pinners, and they had their red brushes and patches from Mademoiselle de la Poche.

Cinderella was likewise called up to them to be consulted in all these matters, for she had excellent notions, and advised them always for the best, nay, and offered her services to dress their heads, which they were very willing she should do. As she was doing this, they said to her:

"Cinderella, would you not be glad to go to the ball?"

"Alas!" said she, "you only jeer me; it is not for such as I am to go thither."

Cinderella

"Thou art in the right of it," replied they; "it would make the people laugh to see a Cinderwench at a ball."

Anyone but Cinderella would have dressed their heads awry, but she was very good, and dressed them perfectly well. They were almost two days without eating, so much they were transported with joy. They broke above a dozen of laces in trying to be laced up close, that they might have a fine slender shape, and they were continually at their looking-glass. At last the happy day came; they went to Court, and Cinderella followed them with her eyes as long as she could, and when she had lost sight of them, she fell a-crying.

Her godmother, who saw her all in tears, asked her what was the matter.

"I wish I could—I wish I could—" she was not able to speak the rest, being interrupted by her tears and sobbing.

Cinderella

This godmother of hers, who was a fairy, said to her, "Thou wishest thou couldst go to the ball; is it not so?"

"Y—es," cried Cinderella, with a great sigh.

"Well," said her godmother, "be but a good girl, and I will contrive that thou shalt go." Then she took her into her chamber, and said to her, "Run into the garden, and bring me a pumpkin."

Cinderella went immediately to gather the finest she could get, and brought it to her godmother, not being able to imagine how this pumpkin could make her go to the ball. Her godmother scooped out all the inside of it, having left nothing but the rind; which done, she struck it with her wand, and the pumpkin was instantly turned into a fine coach, gilded all over with gold.

She then went to look into her mousetrap, where she found six mice, all alive, and ordered Cinderella to lift up a little the trapdoor, when, giving each mouse, as it went out, a little tap with her wand, the mouse was that moment turned into a fine horse, which altogether made a very fine set of six horses of a beautiful mouse-colored dapple-gray. Being at a loss for a coachman,

"I will go and see," says Cinderella, "if there is never a rat in the rat-trap—we may make a coachman of him."

"Thou art in the right," replied her godmother; "go and look."

Cinderella brought the trap to her, and in it there were three huge rats. The fairy made choice of one of the three which had the largest beard, and, having touched him with her wand, he was turned into a fat, jolly coachman, who had the smartest whiskers eyes ever beheld. After that, she said to her:

"Go again into the garden, and you will find six lizards behind the watering-pot, bring them to me."

She had no sooner done so but her godmother turned them into six footmen, who skipped up immediately behind the coach, with their liveries all bedaubed with gold and silver, and clung as close behind each other as if they had done nothing else their whole lives. The fairy then said to Cinderella:

"Well, you see here an equipage fit to go to the ball with; are you not pleased with it?"

"Oh! yes," cried she; "but must I go thither as I am, in these nasty rags?"

Her godmother only just touched her with her wand, and, at the same instant, her clothes were turned into cloth of gold and silver, all beset with jewels. This done, she gave her a pair of glass slippers, the prettiest in the whole world. Being thus decked out, she got up into her coach; but her godmother, above all things, commanded her not to stay till after midnight, telling her, at the same time, that if she stayed one moment longer, the coach would be a pumpkin again, her horses mice, her coachman a rat, her footmen lizards, and her clothes become just as they were before.

She promised her godmother she would not fail of leaving the ball before midnight; and then away she drives, scarce able to contain herself for joy. The King's son, who was told that a great princess, whom nobody knew, was come, ran out to receive her; he gave her his hand as she alighted out of the coach, and led her into the hall, among all the company. There was immediately a profound silence, they left off dancing, and the violins ceased to play, so attentive was everyone to contemplate the singular beauties of the unknown newcomer. Nothing was then heard but a confused noise of:

"Ha! how handsome she is! Ha! how handsome she is!"

The King himself, old as he was, could not help watching her, and telling the Queen softly that it was a long time since he had seen so beautiful and lovely a creature.

Cinderella

All the ladies were busied in considering her clothes and headdress, that they might have some made next day after the same pattern, provided they could meet with such fine materials and as able hands to make them.

The King's son conducted her to the most honorable seat, and afterward took her out to dance with him; she danced so very gracefully that they all more and more admired her. A fine collation was served up, whereof the young prince ate not a morsel, so intently was he busied in gazing on her.

She went and sat down by her sisters, showing them a thousand civilities, giving them part of the oranges and citrons which the Prince had presented her with, which very much surprised them, for they did not know her. While Cinderella was thus amusing her sisters, she heard the clock strike eleven and three-quarters, whereupon she immediately made a courtesy to the company and hasted away as fast as she could.

Being got home, she ran to seek out her godmother, and, after having thanked her, she said she could not but heartily wish she might go next day to the ball, because the King's son had desired her.

As she was eagerly telling her godmother whatever had passed at the ball, her two sisters knocked at the door, which Cinderella ran and opened.

"How long you have stayed!" cried she, gaping, rubbing her eyes and stretching herself as if she had been just waked out of her sleep; she had not, however, any manner of inclination to sleep since they went from home.

"If thou hadst been at the ball," says one of her sisters, "thou wouldst not have been tired with it. There came thither the finest princess, the most beautiful ever was seen with mortal eyes; she showed us a thousand civilities, and gave us oranges and citrons."

Cinderella seemed very indifferent in the matter; indeed, she asked them the name of that princess; but they told her they did not know it, and that the King's son was very uneasy on her account and would give all the world to know who she was. At this Cinderella, smiling, replied:

"She must, then, be very beautiful indeed; how happy you have been! Could not I see her? Ah! dear Miss Charlotte, do lend me your yellow suit of clothes which you wear every day."

"Ay, to be sure!" cried Miss Charlotte; "lend my clothes to such a dirty Cinderwench as thou art! I should be a fool."

Cinderella, indeed, expected well such an answer, and was very glad of the refusal; for she would have been sadly put to it if her sister had lent her what she asked for jestingly.

The next day the two sisters were at the ball, and so was Cinderella, but dressed more magnificently than before. The King's son was always by her, and never ceased his compliments and kind speeches to her; to whom all this was so far from being tiresome that she quite forgot what her godmother had recommended to her; so that she, at last, counted the clock striking twelve when she took it to be no more than eleven; she then rose up and fled, as nimble as a deer. The Prince followed, but could not overtake her. She left behind one of her glass slippers, which the Prince took up most carefully. She got home, but quite out of breath, and in her nasty old clothes, having nothing left of all her finery but one of the little slippers, fellow to that she dropped. The guards at the palace gate were asked:

If they had not seen a princess go out.

Who said: They had seen nobody go out but a young girl, very meanly dressed, and who had more the air of a poor country wench than a gentlewoman.

When the two sisters returned from the ball Cinderella asked them: If they had been well diverted, and if the fine lady had been there.

Cinderella

They told her: Yes, but that she hurried away immediately when it struck twelve, and with so much haste that she dropped one of her little glass slippers, the prettiest in the world, which the King's son had taken up; that he had done nothing but look at her all the time at the ball, and that most certainly he was very much in love with the beautiful person who owned the glass slipper.

What they said was very true; for a few days after the King's son caused it to be proclaimed, by sound of trumpet, that he would marry her whose foot this slipper would just fit. They whom he employed began to try it upon the princesses, then the duchesses and all the Court, but in vain; it was brought to the two sisters, who did all they possibly could to thrust their foot into the slipper, but they could not effect it. Cinderella, who saw all this, and knew her slipper, said to them, laughing:

"Let me see if it will not fit me."

Her sisters burst out laughing, and began to banter her. The gentleman who was sent to try the slipper looked earnestly at Cinderella, and, finding her very handsome, said:

It was but just that she should try, and that he had orders to let everyone make trial.

He obliged Cinderella to sit down, and, putting the slipper to her foot, he found it went on very easily, and fitted her as if it had been made of wax. The astonishment her two sisters were in was excessively great, but still abundantly greater when Cinderella pulled out of her pocket the other slipper, and put it on her foot. Thereupon, in came her godmother, who, having touched with her wand Cinderella's clothes, made them richer and more magnificent than any of those she had before.

And now her two sisters found her to be that fine, beautiful lady whom they had seen at the ball. They threw themselves at her feet to beg pardon for all the ill-treatment they had made her undergo. Cinderella took them up, and, as she embraced them, cried:

That she forgave them with all her heart, and desired them always to love her.

She was conducted to the young Prince, dressed as she was; he thought her more charming than ever, and, a few days after, married her. Cinderella, who was no less good than beautiful, gave her two sisters lodgings in the palace, and that very same day matched them with two great lords of the Court.

The Ratcatcher

A VERY LONG TIME AGO the town of Hamel in Germany was invaded by bands of rats, the like of which had never been seen before nor will ever be again.

They were great black creatures that ran boldly in broad daylight through the streets, and swarmed so, all over the houses, that people at last could not put their hand or foot down anywhere without touching one. When dressing in the morning they found them in their breeches and petticoats, in their pockets and in their boots; and when they wanted a morsel to eat, the voracious horde had swept away everything from cellar to garret. The night was even worse. As soon as the lights were out, these untiring nibblers set to work. And everywhere, in the ceilings, in the floors, in the cupboards, at the doors, there was a chase and a rummage, and so furious a noise of gimlets, pincers, and saws, that a deaf man could not have rested for one hour together.

Neither cats nor dogs, nor poison nor traps, nor prayers nor candles burned to all the saints—nothing would do anything. The more they killed the more came. And the inhabitants of Hamel began to go to the dogs (not that *they* were of much use), when one Friday there arrived in the town a man with a queer face, who played the bagpipes and sang this refrain:

The Ratcatcher

"Qui vivra verra:
Le voilà,
Le preneur des rats."

He was a great gawky fellow, dry and bronzed, with a crooked nose, a long rattail mustache, two great yellow piercing and mocking eyes, under a large felt hat set off by a scarlet cock's feather. He was dressed in a green jacket with a leather belt and red breeches, and on his feet were sandals fastened by thongs passed around his legs in the gypsy fashion.

That is how he may be seen to this day, painted on a window of the cathedral of Hamel.

He stopped on the great marketplace before the town hall, turned his back on the church and went on with his music, singing:

"Who lives shall see:
This is he,
The ratcatcher."

The town council had just assembled to consider once more this plague of Egypt, from which no one could save the town.

The stranger sent word to the counselors that, if they would make it worth his while, he would rid them of all their rats before night, down to the very last.

"Then he is a sorcerer!" cried the citizens with one voice; "we must beware of him."

The Town Counselor, who was considered clever, reassured them.

He said: "Sorcerer or no, if this bagpiper speaks the truth, it was he who sent us this horrible vermin that he wants to rid us of today for money. Well, we must learn to catch the devil in his own snares. You leave it to me."

"Leave it to the Town Counselor," said the citizens one to another.

And the stranger was brought before them.

"Before night," said he, "I shall have dispatched all the rats in Hamel if you will but pay me a *gros* a head."

"A *gros* a head!" cried the citizens, "but that will come to millions of florins!"

The Town Counselor simply shrugged his shoulders and said to the stranger:

"A bargain! To work; the rats will be paid one *gros* a head as you ask."

The bagpiper announced that he would operate that very evening when the moon rose. He added that the inhabitants should at that hour leave the streets free, and content themselves with looking out of their windows at what was passing, and that it would be a pleasant spectacle. When the people of Hamel heard of the bargain, they too exclaimed: "A *gros* a head! But this will cost us a deal of money!"

"Leave it to the Town Counselor," said the town council with a malicious air. And the good people of Hamel repeated with their counselors, "Leave it to the Town Counselor."

Toward nine at night the bagpiper reappeared on the marketplace. He turned, as at first, his back to the church, and the moment the moon rose on the horizon, "Trarira, trari!" the bagpiper resounded.

It was first a slow, caressing sound, then more and more lively and urgent, and so sonorous and piercing that it penetrated as far as the farthest alleys and retreats of the town.

Soon from the bottom of the cellars, the top of the garrets, from under all the furniture, from all the nooks and corners of the houses, out come the rats, search for the door, fling themselves into the street, and trip, trip, trip, begin to run in file toward the front of the town hall, so squeezed together that they covered the pavement like the waves of flooded torrent.

When the square was quite full the bagpiper faced about, and, still playing briskly, turned toward the river that runs at the foot of the walls of Hamel.

Arrived there he turned around; the rats were following.

"Hop! hop!" he cried, pointing with his finger to the middle of the stream, where the water whirled and was drawn down as if through a funnel. And hop! hop! without hesitating, the rats took the leap, swam straight to the funnel, plunged in head foremost and disappeared.

The plunging continued thus without ceasing till midnight.

At last, dragging himself with difficulty, came a big rat, white with age, and stopped on the bank.

It was the king of the band.

"Are they all there, friend Blanchet?" asked the bagpiper.

"They are all there," replied friend Blanchet.

"And how many were they?"

"Nine hundred and ninety thousand, nine hundred and ninety-nine."

"Well reckoned?"

"Well reckoned."

"Then go and join them, old sire, and *au revoir*."

Then the old white rat sprang in his turn into the river, swam to the whirlpool and disappeared.

When the bagpiper had thus concluded his business he went to bed at his inn. And for the first time during three months the people of Hamel slept quietly through the night.

The Ratcatcher

The next morning, at nine o'clock, the bagpiper repaired to the town hall, where the town council awaited him.

"All your rats took a jump into the river yesterday," said he to the counselors, "and I guarantee that not one of them comes back. They were nine hundred and ninety thousand, nine hundred and ninety-nine, at one *gros* a head. Reckon!"

"Let us reckon the heads first. One *gros* a head is one head the *gros*. Where are the heads?"

The ratcatcher did not expect this treacherous stroke. He paled with anger and his eyes flashed fire.

"The heads!" cried he, "if you care about them, go and find them in the river."

"So," replied the Town Counselor, "you refuse to hold to the terms of your agreement? We ourselves could refuse you all payment. But you have been of use to us, and we will not let you go without a recompense," and he offered him fifty crowns.

"Keep your recompense for yourself," replied the ratcatcher proudly. "If you do not pay me I will be paid by your heirs."

Thereupon he pulled his hat down over his eyes, went hastily out of the hall, and left the town without speaking to a soul.

When the Hamel people heard how the affair had ended they rubbed their hands, and with no more scruple than their Town Counselor, they laughed over the ratcatcher, who, they said, was caught in his own trap. But what made them laugh above all was his threat of getting himself paid by their heirs. Ha! they wished that they only had such creditors for the rest of their lives.

Next day, which was a Sunday, they all went gaily to church, thinking that after Mass they would at last be able to eat some good thing that the rats had not tasted before them.

The Ratcatcher

They never suspected the terrible surprise that awaited them on their return home. No children anywhere, they had all disappeared!

"Our children! Where are our poor children?" was the cry that was soon heard in all the streets.

Then through the east door of the town came three little boys, who cried and wept, and this is what they told:

While the parents were at church a wonderful music had resounded. Soon all the little boys and all the little girls that had been left at home had gone out, attracted by the magic sounds, and had rushed to the great marketplace. There they found the ratcatcher playing his bagpipes at the same spot as the evening before. Then the stranger had begun to walk quickly, and they had followed, running, singing and dancing to the sound of the music, as far as the foot of the mountain which one sees on entering Hamel. At their approach the mountain had opened a little, and the bagpiper had gone in with them, after which it had closed again. Only the three little ones who told the

adventure had remained outside, as if by a miracle. One was bandy-legged and could not run fast enough; the other, who had left the house in haste, one foot shod the other bare, had hurt himself against a big stone and could not walk without difficulty; the third had arrived in time, but in hurrying to go in with the others had struck so violently against the wall of the mountain that he fell backward at the moment it closed upon his comrades.

At this story the parents redoubled their lamentations. They ran with pikes and mattocks to the mountain, and searched till evening to find the opening by which their children had disappeared, without being able to find it. At last, the night falling, they returned desolate to Hamel.

But the most unhappy of all was the Town Counselor, for he lost three little boys and two pretty little girls, and to crown all, the people of Hamel overwhelmed him with reproaches, forgetting that the evening before they had all agreed with him.

What had become of all these unfortunate children?

The parents always hoped they were not dead, and that the ratcatcher, who certainly must have come out of the mountain, would have taken them with him to his country. That is why for several years they sent in search of them to different countries, but no one ever came on the trace of the poor little ones.

It was not till much later that anything was to be heard of them.

About one hundred and fifty years after the event, when there was no longer one left of the fathers, mothers, brothers or sisters of that day, there arrived one evening in Hamel some merchants of Bremen returning from the East, who asked to speak with the citizens. They told that they, in crossing Hungary, had sojourned in a mountainous country called Transylvania, where the inhabitants only spoke German, while all around them nothing was spoken but Hungarian. These people also declared that they came from Germany, but they did not know how they chanced to be in this strange country. "Now," said the merchants of Bremen, "these Germans cannot be other than the descendants of the lost children of Hamel."

The people of Hamel did not doubt it; and since that day they regard it as certain that the Transylvanians of Hungary are their country folk, whose ancestors, as children, were brought there by the ratcatcher. There are more difficult things to believe than that.

The Fisherman and His Wife

❦

THERE WAS ONCE a fisherman and his wife who lived together in a little hut close to the sea, and the fisherman used to go down every day to fish; and he would fish and fish. So he used to sit with his rod and gaze into the shining water; and he would gaze and gaze.

Now, once the line was pulled deep under the water, and when he hauled it up he hauled a large flounder with it. The flounder said to him, "Listen, fisherman. I pray you to let me go; I am not a real flounder, I am an enchanted prince. What good will it do you if you kill me—I shall not taste nice? Put me back into the water and let me swim away."

"Well," said the man, "you need not make so much noise about it; I am sure I had much better let a flounder that can talk swim away." With these words he put him back again into the shining water, and the flounder sank to the bottom, leaving a long streak of blood behind. Then the fisherman got up, and went home to his wife in the hut.

"Husband," said his wife, "have you caught nothing today?"

"No," said the man. "I caught a flounder who said he was an enchanted prince, so I let him swim away again."

"Did you wish nothing from him?" said his wife.

"No," said the man; "what should I have wished from him?"

44

The Fisherman and His Wife

"Ah!" said the woman, "it's dreadful to have to live all one's life in this hut that is so small and dirty; you ought to have wished for a cottage. Go now and call him; say to him that we choose to have a cottage, and he will certainly give it you."

"Alas!" said the man, "why should I go down there again?"

"Why," said his wife, "you caught him, and then let him go again, so he is sure to give you what you ask. Go down quickly."

The man did not like going at all, but as his wife was not to be persuaded, he went down to the sea.

When he came there the sea was quite green and yellow, and was no longer shining. So he stood on the shore and said:

> *"Once a prince, but changed you be*
> *Into a flounder in the sea.*
> *Come! for my wife, Ilsebel,*
> *Wishes what I dare not tell."*

Then the flounder came swimming up and said, "Well, what does she want?"

"Alas!" said the man, "my wife says I ought to have kept you and wished something from you. She does not want to live any longer in the hut; she would like a cottage."

"Go home, then," said the flounder; "she has it."

So the man went home, and there was his wife no longer in the hut, but in its place was a beautiful cottage, and his wife was sitting in front of the door on a bench. She took him by the hand and said to him, "Come inside, and see if this is not much better." They went in, and inside the cottage was a tiny hall, and a beautiful sitting room, and a bedroom in which stood a bed, a kitchen and a dining room all furnished with the best of everything, and fitted up with every kind of tin and copper utensil. And outside was a little yard in which were chickens and ducks, and also a little garden with vegetables and fruit trees.

"See," said the wife, "isn't this nice?"

"Yes," answered her husband; "here we shall remain and live very happily."

"We will think about that," said his wife.

With these words they had their supper and went to bed. All went well for a week or a fortnight, then the wife said:

"Listen, husband; the cottage is much too small, and so is the yard and the garden; the flounder might just as well have sent us a larger house. I should like to live in a great stone castle. Go down to the flounder, and tell him to send us a castle."

"Ah, wife!" said the fisherman, "the cottage is quite good enough; why do we choose to live in a castle?"

"Why?" said the wife. "You go down; the flounder can quite well do that."

"No, wife," said the man; "the flounder gave us the cottage. I do not like to go to him again; he might take it amiss."

"Go," said his wife. "He can certainly give it us, and ought to do so willingly. Go at once."

The fisherman's heart was very heavy, and he did not like going. He said to himself, "It is not right." Still, he went down.

When he came to the sea, the water was all violet and dark blue, and dull and thick, and no longer green and yellow, but it was still smooth.

So he stood there and said:

> *"Once a prince, but changed you be*
> *Into a flounder in the sea.*
> *Come! for my wife, Ilsebel,*
> *Wishes what I dare not tell."*

"What does she want now?" said the flounder.

"Ah!" said the fisherman, half-ashamed, "she wants to live in a great stone castle."

"Go home; she is standing before the door," said the flounder.

The fisherman went home and thought he would find no house. When he came near, there stood a great stone palace, and his wife was standing on the steps, about to enter. She took him by the hand and said, "Come inside."

Then he went with her, and inside the castle was a large hall with a marble floor, and there were heaps of servants who threw open the great doors, and the walls were covered with beautiful tapestry, and in the apartments were gilded chairs and tables, and crystal chandeliers hung from the ceiling, and all the rooms were beautifully carpeted. The best of food and drink also was set before them when they wished to dine. And outside the house was a large courtyard with horse and cow stables and a coach-house—all fine buildings; and a splendid garden with most beautiful flowers and fruit, and in a park quite a league long were deer and roe and hares, and everything one could wish for.

"Now," said the wife, "isn't this beautiful?"

"Yes, indeed," said the fisherman. "Now we will stay here and live in this beautiful castle, and be very happy."

"We will consider the matter," said his wife, and they went to bed.

The next morning the wife woke up first at daybreak, and looked out of the bed at the beautiful country stretched before her. Her husband was still sleeping, so she dug her elbows into his side and said:

"Husband, get up and look out of the window. Could we not become the king of all this land? Go down to the flounder and tell him we choose to be king."

"Ah, wife!" replied her husband, "why should we be king? *I* don't want to be king."

"Well," said his wife, "if you don't want to be king, *I* will be king. Go down to the flounder; I will be king."

"Alas! wife," said the fisherman, "why do you want to be king? I can't ask him that."

"And why not?" said his wife. "Go down at once. I must be king."

So the fisherman went, though much vexed that his wife wanted to be king. "It is not right! It is not right," he thought. He did not wish to go, yet he went.

When he came to the sea, the water was a dark-gray color, and it was heaving against the shore. So he stood and said:

"Once a prince, but changed you be
Into a flounder in the sea.

The Fisherman and His Wife

Come! for my wife, Ilsebel,
Wishes what I dare not tell."

"What does she want now?" asked the flounder.

"Alas!" said the fisherman, "she wants to be king."

"Go home; she is that already," said the flounder.

The fisherman went home, and when he came near the palace he saw that it had become much larger, and that it had great towers and splendid ornamental carving on it. A sentinel was standing before the gate, and there were numbers of soldiers with kettledrums and trumpets. And when he went into the palace, he found everything was of pure marble and gold, and the curtains of damask with tassels of gold. Then the doors of the hall flew open, and there stood the whole Court around his wife, who was sitting on a high throne of gold and diamonds; she wore a great golden crown, and had a scepter of gold and precious stones in her hand, and by her on either side stood six pages in a row, each one a head taller than the other. Then he went before her and said:

"Ah, wife! are you king now?"

"Yes," said his wife; "now I am king."

He stood looking at her, and when he had looked for some time, he said:

"Let that be enough, wife, now that you are king! Now we have nothing more to wish for."

"Nay, husband," said his wife restlessly, "my wishing powers are boundless; I cannot restrain them any longer. Go down to the flounder; king I am, now I must be emperor."

"Alas! wife," said the fisherman, "why do you want to be emperor?"

"Husband," said she, "go to the flounder; I *will* be emperor."

"Ah, wife," he said, "he cannot make you emperor; I don't like to ask him that. There is only one emperor in the kingdom. Indeed and indeed he cannot make you emperor."

"What!" said his wife. "I am king, and you are my husband. Will you go at once? Go! If he can make king he can make emperor, and emperor I must and will be. Go!"

So he had to go. But as he went, he felt quite frightened, and he thought to himself, "This can't be right; to be emperor is too ambitious; the flounder will be tired out at last."

Thinking this he came to the shore. The sea was quite black and thick, and it was breaking high on the beach; the foam was flying about, and the wind was blowing; everything looked bleak. The fisherman was chilled with fear. He stood and said:

"Once a prince, but changed you be
Into a flounder in the sea.
Come! for my wife, Ilsebel,
Wishes what I dare not tell."

"What does she want now?" asked the flounder.

"Alas! flounder," he said, "my wife wants to be emperor."

"Go home," said the flounder; "she is that already."

So the fisherman went home, and when he came there he saw the whole castle was made of polished marble, ornamented with alabaster statues and gold. Before the gate soldiers were marching, blowing trumpets and beating drums. Inside the palace were walking barons, counts, and dukes, acting as servants; they opened the door, which was of beaten gold. And when he entered, he saw his wife upon a throne which was made out of a single block of gold, and which was quite six cubits high. She had on a great golden crown which was three yards high and set with brilliants and sparkling gems. In one hand she held a scepter, and in the other the imperial globe, and on either side of her stood two rows of halberdiers, each smaller than the other, from a seven-foot giant to the tiniest little dwarf no higher than my little finger. Many princes and dukes were standing before her. The fisherman went up to her quietly and said:

"Wife, are you emperor now?"

"Yes," she said, "I am emperor."

He stood looking at her magnificence, and when he had watched her for some time, said:

"Ah, wife, let that be enough, now that you are emperor."

"Husband," said she, "why are you standing there? I am emperor now, and I want to be pope too; go down to the flounder."

"Alas! wife," said the fisherman, "what more do you want? You cannot be pope; there is only one pope in Christendom, and he cannot make you that."

"Husband," she said, "I *will* be pope. Go down quickly; I must be pope today."

"No, wife," said the fisherman; "I can't ask him that. It is not right; it is too much. The flounder cannot make you pope."

"Husband, what nonsense!" said his wife. "If he can make emperor, he can make pope too. Go down this instant; I am emperor and you are my husband. Will you be off at once?"

So he was frightened and went out; but he felt quite faint, and trembled and shook, and his knees and legs began to give way under him. The wind was blowing fiercely across the land, and the clouds flying across the sky looked as gloomy as if it were night; the leaves were being blown from the trees; the water was foaming and seething and dashing upon the shore, and in the distance he saw the ships in great distress, dancing and tossing on the waves. Still the sky was very blue in the middle, although at the sides it was an angry red as in a great storm. So he stood shuddering in anxiety, and said:

"Once a prince, but changed you be
Into a flounder in the sea.
Come! for my wife, Ilsebel,
Wishes what I dare not tell."

"Well, what does she want now?" asked the flounder.

"Alas!" said the fisherman, "she wants to be pope."

"Go home, then; she is that already," said the flounder.

Then he went home, and when he came there he saw, as it were, a large church surrounded by palaces. He pushed his way through the people. The interior was lit up with thousands and thousands of candles, and his wife was dressed in cloth of gold and was sitting on a much higher throne, and she wore three great golden crowns. Around her were numbers of Church dignitaries, and on either side were standing two rows of tapers, the largest of them as tall as a steeple, and the smallest as tiny as a Christmas-tree candle. All the emperors and kings were on their knees before her, and were kissing her foot.

"Wife," said the fisherman looking at her, "are you pope now?"

"Yes," said she; "I am pope."

So he stood staring at her, and it was as if he were looking at the bright sun. When he had watched her for some time he said: "Ah, wife, let it be enough now that you are pope."

But she sat as straight as a tree, and did not move or bend the least bit. He said again:

"Wife, be content now that you are pope. You cannot become anything more."

"We will think about that," said his wife.

With these words they went to bed. But the woman was not content; her greed would not allow her to sleep, and she kept on thinking and thinking what she could still become. The fisherman slept well and soundly, for he had done a great deal that day, but his wife could not sleep at all, and turned from one side to another the whole night long, and thought, till she could think no longer, what more she could become. Then the sun began to rise, and when she saw the red dawn she went to the end of the bed and looked at it, and as she was watching the sun rise, out of the window, she thought, "Ha! could I not make the sun and man rise?"

"Husband," said she, poking him in the ribs with her elbows, "wake up. Go down to the flounder; I will be a god."

The fisherman was still half asleep, yet he was so frightened that he fell out of bed. He thought he had not heard aright, and opened his eyes wide and said:

"What did you say, wife?"

"Husband," she said, "if I cannot make the sun and man rise when I appear I cannot rest. I shall never have a quiet moment till I can make the sun and man rise."

He looked at her in horror, and a shudder ran over him.

"Go down at once; I will be a god."

"Alas! wife," said the fisherman, falling on his knees before her, "the flounder cannot do that. Emperor and pope he can make you. I implore you, be content and remain pope."

Then she flew into a passion, her hair hung wildly about her face, she pushed him with her foot and screamed:

"I am not contented, and I shall not be contented! Will you go?"

So he hurried on his clothes as fast as possible, and ran away as if he were mad.

But the storm was raging so fiercely that he could scarcely stand. Houses and trees were being blown down, the mountains were being shaken, and pieces of rock were rolling in the sea. The sky was as black as ink, it was thundering and lightening, and the sea was tossing in great waves as high as church towers and mountains, and each had a white crest of foam.

So he shouted, not able to hear his own voice:

> *"Once a prince, but changed you be*
> *Into a flounder in the sea.*
> *Come! for my wife, Ilsebel,*
> *Wishes what I dare not tell."*

"Well, what does she want now?" asked the flounder.

"Alas!" said he, "she wants to be a god."

"Go home, then; she is sitting again in the hut."

And there they are sitting to this day.

The Swineherd

THERE WAS ONCE a poor prince. He possessed a kingdom which, though small, was yet large enough for him to marry on, and married he wished to be.

Now it was certainly a little audacious of him to venture to say to the Emperor's daughter, "Will you marry me?" But he did venture to say so, for his name was known far and wide. There were hundreds of princesses who would gladly have said "Yes," but would she say the same?

Well, we shall see.

On the grave of the Prince's father grew a rose tree, a very beautiful rose tree. It only bloomed every five years, and then bore but a single rose, but oh, such a rose! Its scent was so sweet that when you smelled it you forgot all your cares and troubles. And he had also a nightingale which could sing as if all the beautiful melodies in the world were shut up in its little throat. This rose and this nightingale the Princess was to have, and so they were both put into silver caskets and sent to her.

The Emperor had them brought to him in the great hall, where the Princess was playing "Here comes a duke a-riding" with her ladies-in-waiting. And when she caught sight of the big caskets which contained the presents, she clapped her hands for joy.

"If only it were a little pussycat," she said. But the rose tree with the beautiful rose came out.

"But how prettily it is made!" said all the ladies-in-waiting.

"It is more than pretty," said the Emperor, "it is charming!"

But the Princess felt it, and then she almost began to cry.

"Ugh! Papa," she said, "it is not artificial, it is *real*!"

"Ugh!" said all the ladies-in-waiting, "it is real!"

"Let us see first what is in the other casket before we begin to be angry," thought the Emperor, and there came out the nightingale. It sang so beautifully that one could scarcely utter a cross word against it.

"*Superbe! charmant!*" said the ladies-in-waiting, for they all chattered French, each one worse than the other.

"How much the bird reminds me of the musical snuffbox of the late Empress!" said an old courtier. "Ah, yes, it is the same tone, the same execution!"

"Yes," said the Emperor; and then he wept like a little child.

"I hope that this, at least, is not real?" asked the Princess.

"Yes, it is a real bird," said those who had brought it.

"Then let the bird fly away," said the Princess; and she would not on any account allow the Prince to come.

"But he was nothing daunted. He painted his face, drew his cap well over his face, and knocked at the door. "Good-day, Emperor," he said. "Can I get a place here as servant in the castle?"

"Yes," said the Emperor, "but there are so many who ask for a place that I don't know whether there will be one for you; but, still, I will think of you. Stay, it has just occurred to me that I want someone to look after the swine, for I have so very many of them."

And the Prince got the situation of Imperial Swineherd. He had a wretched little room close to the pigsties; here he had to stay, but the whole day he sat working, and when evening was come he had made a pretty little pot. All around it were little bells, and when the pot boiled they jingled most beautifully and played the old tune—

The Swineherd

"Where is Augustus dear?
Alas! he's not here, here, here!"

But the most wonderful thing was, that when one held one's finger in the steam of the pot, then at once one could smell what dinner was ready in any fireplace in the town. That was indeed something quite different from the rose.

Now the Princess came walking past with all her ladies-in-waiting, and when she heard the tune she stood still and her face beamed with joy, for she too could play "Where is Augustus dear?"

It was the only tune she knew, but that she could play with one finger.

"Why, that is what I play!" she said. "He must be a most accomplished Swineherd! Listen! Go down and ask him what the instrument costs."

And one of the ladies-in-waiting had to go down; but she put on wooden clogs. "What will you take for the pot?" asked the lady-in-waiting.

"I will have ten kisses from the Princess," answered the Swineherd.

"Heaven forbid!" said the lady-in-waiting.

"Yes, I will sell it for nothing less," replied the Swineherd.

"Well, what does he say?" asked the Princess.

"I really hardly like to tell you," answered the lady-in-waiting.

"Oh, then you can whisper it to me."

"He is disobliging!" said the Princess, and went away. But she had only gone a few steps when the bells rang out so prettily—

"Where is Augustus dear?
Alas! he's not here, here, here!"

58

The Swineherd

"Listen!" said the Princess. "Ask him whether he will take ten kisses from my ladies-in-waiting."

"No, thank you," said the Swineherd. "Ten kisses from the Princess, or else I keep my pot."

"That is very tiresome!" said the Princess. "But you must put yourselves in front of me, so that no one can see."

And the ladies-in-waiting placed themselves in front and then spread out their dresses; so the Swineherd got his ten kisses, and she got the pot.

What happiness that was! The whole night and the whole day the pot was made to boil; there was not a fireplace in the whole town where they did not know what was being cooked, whether it was at the chancellor's or at the shoemaker's.

The ladies-in-waiting danced and clapped their hands.

"We know who is going to have soup and pancakes; we know who is going to have porridge and sausages—isn't it interesting?"

"Yes, very interesting!" said the first lady-in-waiting.

"But don't say anything about it, for I am the Emperor's daughter."

"Oh, no, of course we won't!" said everyone.

The Swineherd—that is to say, the Prince (though they did not know he was anything but a true Swineherd)—let no day pass without making something, and one day he made a rattle which, when it was turned around, played all the waltzes, galops, and polkas which had ever been known since the world began.

"But that is *superbe!*" said the Princess as she passed by. "I have never heard a more beautiful composition. Listen! Go down and ask him what this instrument costs; but I won't kiss him again."

"He wants a hundred kisses from the Princess," said the lady-in-waiting who had gone down to ask him.

The Swineherd

"I believe he is mad!" said the Princess, and then she went on; but she had only gone a few steps when she stopped.

"One ought to encourage art," she said. "I am the Emperor's daughter! Tell him he shall have, as before, ten kisses; the rest he can take from my ladies-in-waiting."

"But we don't at all like being kissed by him," said the ladies-in-waiting.

"That's nonsense," said the Princess; "and if I can kiss him, you can too. Besides, remember that I give you board and lodging."

So the ladies-in-waiting had to go down to him again.

"A hundred kisses from the Princess," said he, "or each keeps his own."

"Put yourselves in front of us," she said then; and so all the ladies-in-waiting put themselves in front, and he began to kiss the Princess.

"What can that commotion be by the pigsties?" asked the Emperor, who was standing on the balcony. He rubbed his eyes and put on his spectacles. "Why those are the ladies-in-waiting playing their games; I must go down to them."

So he took off his shoes, which were shoes though he had trodden them down into slippers. What a hurry he was in, to be sure!

As soon as he came into the yard he walked very softly, and the ladies-in-waiting were so busy counting the kisses and seeing fair play that they never noticed the Emperor. He stood on tiptoe.

"What is that?" he said, when he saw the kissing; and then he threw one of his slippers at their heads just as the Swineherd was taking his eighty-sixth kiss.

"Be off with you!" said the Emperor, for he was very angry. And the Princess and the Swineherd were driven out of the empire.

The Swineherd

Then she stood still and wept; the Swineherd was scolding, and the rain was streaming down.

"Alas, what an unhappy creature I am!" sobbed the Princess. "If only I had taken the beautiful Prince! Alas, how unfortunate I am!"

And the Swineherd went behind a tree, washed the paint off his face, threw away his old clothes, and then stepped forward in his splendid dress, looking so beautiful that the Princess was obliged to courtesy.

"I now come to this. I despise you!" he said. "You would have nothing to do with a noble Prince; you did not understand the rose or the nightingale, but you could kiss the Swineherd for the sake of a toy. This is what you get for it!" And he went into his kingdom and shut the door in her face, and she had to stay outside singing—

"Where is Augustus dear?
Alas! he's not here, here, here!"

Rumpelstiltzkin

❦

THERE WAS ONCE UPON A TIME a poor miller who
had a very beautiful daughter. Now it happened one day that he
had an audience with the King, and in order to appear a person of some
importance he told him that he had a daughter who could spin straw
into gold. "Now that's a talent worth having," said the King to the
miller; "if your daughter is as clever as you say, bring her to my palace
tomorrow, and I'll put her to the test." When the girl was brought to
him he led her into a room full of straw, gave her a spinning wheel and
spindle, and said: "Now set to work and spin all night till early dawn,
and if by that time you haven't spun the straw into gold you shall die."
Then he closed the door behind him and left her alone inside.

So the poor miller's daughter sat down, and didn't know what in the
world she was to do. She hadn't the least idea of how to spin straw into
gold, and became at last so miserable that she began to cry. Suddenly
the door opened, and in stepped a tiny little man and said: "Good
evening, Miss Miller-maid; why are you crying so bitterly?" "Oh!" answered the girl, "I have to spin straw into gold, and haven't a notion
how it's done." "What will you give me if I spin it for you?" asked the
manikin. "My necklace," replied the girl. The little man took the necklace, sat himself down at the wheel, and whir, whir, whir, the wheel
went around three times, and the bobbin was full. Then he put on

another, and whir, whir, whir, the wheel went around three times, and the second too was full; and so it went on till the morning, when all the straw was spun away, and all the bobbins were full of gold. As soon as the sun rose the King came, and when he perceived the gold he was astonished and delighted, but his heart only lusted more than ever after the precious metal. He had the miller's daughter put into another room full of straw, much bigger than the first, and bade her, if she valued her life, spin it all into gold before the following morning. The girl didn't know what to do, and began to cry; then the door opened as before, and the tiny little man appeared and said: "What'll you give me if I spin the straw into gold for you?"

"The ring from any finger," answered the girl. The manikin took the ring, and whir! around went the spinning wheel again, and when

morning broke he had spun all the straw into glittering gold. The King was pleased beyond measure at the sight, but his greed for gold was still not satisfied, and he had the miller's daughter brought into a yet bigger room full of straw, and said: "You must spin all this away in the night; but if you succeed this time you shall become my wife." "She's only a miller's daughter, it's true," he thought; "but I couldn't find a richer wife if I were to search the whole world over." When the girl was alone the little man appeared for the third time, and said: "What'll you give me if I spin the straw for you once again?" "I've nothing more to give," answered the girl. "Then promise me when you are Queen to give me your first child." "Who knows what mayn't happen before that?" thought the miller's daughter; and besides, she saw no other way out of it, so she promised the manikin what he demanded, and he set to work once more and spun the straw into gold. When the King came in the morning, and found everything as he had desired, he straightway made her his wife, and the miller's daughter became a queen.

When a year had passed a beautiful son was born to her, and she thought no more of the little man, till all of a sudden one day he stepped into her room and said: "Now give me what you promised." The Queen was in a great state, and offered the little man all the riches in her kingdom if he would only leave her the child. But the manikin said: "No, a living creature is dearer to me than all the treasures in the world." Then the Queen began to cry and sob so bitterly that the little man was sorry for her, and said: "I'll give you three days to guess my name, and if you find it out in that time you may keep your child."

Then the Queen pondered the whole night over all the names she had ever heard, and sent a messenger to scour the land, and to pick up far and near any names he should come across. When the little man arrived on the following day she began with Kasper, Melchior,

Rumpelstiltzkin

Belshazzar, and all the other names she knew, in a string, but at each one the manikin called out: "That's not my name." The next day she sent to inquire the names of all the people in the neighborhood, and had a long list of the most uncommon and extraordinary for the little man when he made his appearance. "Is your name, perhaps, Sheepshanks, Cruickshanks, Spindleshanks?" but he always replied: "That's not my name." On the third day the messenger returned and announced: "I have not been able to find any new names, but as I came upon a high hill around the corner of the wood, where the foxes and hares bid each other good night, I saw a little house, and in front of the house burned a fire, and around the fire sprang the most grotesque little man, hopping on one leg and crying:

> *"Tomorrow I brew, today I bake,*
> *And then the child away I'll take;*
> *For little deems my royal dame*
> *That Rumpelstiltzkin is my name!"*

You may imagine the Queen's delight at hearing the name, and when the little man stepped in shortly afterward and asked: "Now, my lady Queen, what's my name?" she asked first: "Is your name Conrad?" "No." "Is your name Harry?" "No." "Is your name, perhaps, Rumpelstiltzkin?" "Some demon has told you that, some demon has told you that," screamed the little man, and in his rage drove his right foot so far into the ground that it sank in up to his waist; then in a passion he seized the left foot with both hands and tore himself in two.

The Cunning Hare

IN A VERY COLD COUNTRY, far across the seas, where ice and snow cover the ground for many months in the year, there lived a little hare, who, as his father and mother were both dead, was brought up by his grandmother. As he was too young, and she was too old, to work, they were very poor, and often did not have enough to eat.

One day, when the little fellow was hungrier than usual, he asked his grandmother if he might not go down to the river and catch a fish for their breakfast, as the thaw had come and the water was flowing freely again. She laughed at him for thinking that any fish would let itself be caught by a hare, especially such a young one; but as she had the rheumatism very badly, and could get no food herself, she let him go. "If he does not catch a fish he may find something else," she said to herself. So she told her grandson where to look for the net, and how he was to set it across the river; but just as he was starting, feeling himself quite a man, she called him back.

"After all, I don't know what is the use of your going, my boy! For even if you should catch a fish, I have no fire to cook it with."

"Let me catch my fish, and I will soon make you a fire," he answered gaily, for he was young, and knew nothing about the difficulties of fire-making.

It took him some time to haul the net through bushes and over fields, but at length he reached a pool in the river which he had often heard was swarming with fish, and here he set the net, as his grandmother had directed him.

He was so excited that he hardly slept all night, and at the very first streak of dawn he ran as fast as ever he could down to the river. His heart beat as quickly as if he had had dogs behind him, and he hardly dared to look, lest he should be disappointed. Would there be even one fish? And at this thought the pangs of hunger made him feel quite sick with fear. But he need not have been afraid; in every mesh of the net was a fine fat fish, and of course the net itself was so heavy that he could only lift one corner. He threw some of the fish back into the water, and buried some more in a hole under a stone, where he would be sure to find them. Then he rolled up the net with the rest, put it on his back and carried it home. The weight of the load caused his back to ache, and he was thankful to drop it outside their hut, while he rushed in, full of joy, to tell his grandmother. "Be quick and clean them!" he said, "and I will go to those people's tents on the other side of the water."

The old woman stared at him in horror as she listened to his proposal. Other people had tried to steal fire before, and few indeed had come back with their lives; but as, contrary to all her expectations, he had managed to catch such a number of fish, she thought that perhaps there was some magic about him which she did not know of, and did not try to hinder him.

When the fish were all taken out, he fetched the net which he had laid out to dry, folded it up very small, and ran down to the river, hoping that he might find a place narrow enough for him to jump over; but he soon saw that it was too wide for even the best jumper in the world. For a few moments he stood there, wondering what was to be done, then there darted into his head some words of a spell which he had once heard a wizard use, while drinking from the river. He repeated them, as well as he could remember, and waited to see what would happen. In five minutes such a grunting and a puffing was heard, and columns of water rose into the air, though he could not tell what had made them. Then around the bend of the stream came fifteen huge whales, which he ordered to place themselves heads to tails, like stepping stones, so that he could jump from one to the other till he landed on the opposite shore. Directly he got there he told the whales that he did not need them any more, and sat down in the sand to rest.

The Cunning Hare

Unluckily some children who were playing about caught sight of him, and one of them, stealing softly up behind him, laid tight hold of his ears. The hare, who had been watching the whales as they sailed down the river, gave a violent start, and struggled to get away; but the boy held on tight, and ran back home, as fast as he could go.

"Throw it in the pot," said the old woman, as soon as he had told his story; "put it in that basket, and as soon as the water boils in the pot we will hang it over the fire!"

"Better kill it first," said the old man; and the hare listened, horribly frightened, but still looking secretly to see if there was no hole through which he could escape, if he had a chance of doing so. Yes, there was one, right in the top of the tent, so, shaking himself, as if with fright, he let the end of his net unroll itself a little.

"I wish that a spark of fire would fall on my net," whispered he; and the next minute a great log fell forward into the midst of the tent, causing every one to spring backward. The sparks were scattered in every direction, and one fell on the net, making a little blaze. In an instant the hare had leaped through the hole, and was racing toward the river, with men, women, and children after him. There was no time to call back the whales, so, holding the net tight in his mouth, he wished himself across the river. Then he jumped high into the air, and landed safe on the other side, and after turning around to be sure that there was no chance of anyone pursuing him, trotted happily home to his grandmother.

"Didn't I tell you I would bring you fire?" said he, holding up his net, which was now burning briskly.

"But how did you cross the water?" inquired the old woman.

"Oh, I just jumped!" said he. And his grandmother asked him no more questions, for she saw that he was wiser than she.

The History of
Jack the Giant Killer

❦

IN THE REIGN of the famous King Arthur there lived in Cornwall a lad named Jack, who was a boy of a bold temper, and took delight in hearing or reading of conjurers, giants, and fairies; and used to listen eagerly to the deeds of the knights of King Arthur's Round Table.

In those days there lived on St. Michael's Mount, off Cornwall, a huge giant, eighteen feet high and nine feet around; his fierce and savage looks were the terror of all who beheld him.

He dwelt in a gloomy cavern on the top of the mountain, and used to wade over to the mainland in search of prey; when he would throw half-a-dozen oxen upon his back, and tie three times as many sheep and hogs around his waist, and march back to his own abode.

The giant had done this for many years when Jack resolved to destroy him.

Jack took a horn, a shovel, a pickaxe, his armor, and a dark lantern, and one winter's evening he went to the mount. There he dug a pit twenty-two feet deep and twenty broad. He covered the top over so as to make it look like solid ground. He then blew such a tantivy that the giant awoke and came out of his den, crying out: "You saucy villain! you shall pay for this. I'll broil you for my breakfast!"

He had just finished, when, taking one step further, he tumbled headlong into the pit, and Jack struck him a blow on the head with his pickaxe, which killed him. Jack then returned home to cheer his friends with the news.

Another giant, called Blunderbore, vowed to be revenged on Jack if ever he should have him in his power. This giant kept an enchanted castle in the midst of a lonely wood; and some time after the death of Cormoran Jack was passing through a wood, and being weary sat down and went to sleep.

The giant, passing by and seeing Jack, carried him to his castle, where he locked him up in a large room, the floor of which was covered with the bodies, skulls, and bones of men and women.

Soon after the giant went to fetch his brother, who was likewise a giant, to take a meal off his flesh; and Jack saw with terror through the bars of his prison the two giants approaching.

Jack, perceiving in one corner of the room a strong cord, took courage, and making a slip-knot at each end, he threw them over their heads, and tied it to the window bars; he then pulled till he had choked them. When they were blue in the face he slid down the rope and stabbed them to the heart.

Jack next took a great bunch of keys from the pocket of Blunderbore, and went into the castle again. He made a strict search through all the rooms, and in one of them found three ladies tied up by the hair of their heads, and almost starved to death. They told him that their husbands had been killed by the giants, who had then condemned them to be starved to death, because they would not eat the flesh of their own dead husbands.

"Ladies," said Jack, "I have put an end to the monster and his wicked brother; and I give you this castle and all the riches it contains, to make some amends for the dreadful pains you have felt." He then very politely gave them the keys of the castle, and went further on his journey to Wales.

As Jack had but little money, he went on as fast as possible. At length he came to a handsome house. Jack knocked at the door, when there came forth a Welsh giant. Jack said he was a traveler who had lost his way, on which the giant made him welcome, and let him into a room where there was a good bed to sleep in.

Jack took off his clothes quickly, but though he was weary he could not go to sleep. Soon after this he heard the giant walking backward and forward in the next room, and saying to himself:

> *"Though here you lodge with me this night,*
> *You shall not see the morning light;*
> *My club shall dash your brains out quite."*

"Say you so?" thought Jack. "Are these your tricks upon travelers? But I hope to prove as cunning as you are." Then, getting out of bed, he groped about the room, and at last found a large thick billet of wood. He laid it in his own place in the bed, and then hid himself in a dark corner of the room.

The giant, about midnight, entered the apartment, and with his bludgeon struck a many blows on the bed, in the very place where Jack had laid the log; and then he went back to his own room, thinking he had broken all Jack's bones.

Early in the morning Jack put a bold face upon the matter, and

walked into the giant's room to thank him for his lodging. The giant started when he saw him, and began to stammer out: "Oh! dear me; is it you? Pray how did you sleep last night? Did you hear or see anything in the dead of the night?"

"Nothing worth speaking of," said Jack carelessly: "a rat, I believe, gave me three or four slaps with its tail, and disturbed me a little; but I soon went to sleep again."

The giant wondered more and more at this: yet he did not answer a word, but went to bring two great bowls of hasty-pudding for their breakfast. Jack wanted to make the giant believe that he could eat as much as himself, so he contrived to button a leathern bag inside his coat, and slip the hasty-pudding into this bag, while he seemed to put it into his mouth.

When breakfast was over he said to the giant: "Now I will show you a fine trick. I can cure all wounds with a touch: I could cut off my head in one minute, and the next put it sound again on my shoulders. You shall see an example." He then took hold of the knife, ripped up the leathern bag, and all the hasty-pudding tumbled out upon the floor.

"Ods splutter hur nails!" cried the Welsh giant, who was ashamed to be outdone by such a little fellow as Jack, "hur can do that hurself"; so he snatched up the knife, plunged it into his own stomach, and in a moment dropped down dead.

Jack, having hitherto been successful in all his undertakings, resolved not to be idle in future; he therefore furnished himself with a horse, a cap of knowledge, a sword of sharpness, shoes of swiftness, and an invisible coat, the better to perform the wonderful enterprises that lay before him.

He traveled over high hills, and on the third day he came to a large and spacious forest through which his road lay. Scarcely had he entered the forest when he beheld a monstrous giant dragging along by the hair of their heads a handsome knight and his lady. Jack alighted from his horse, and tying him to an oak tree, put on his invisible coat, under which he carried his sword of sharpness.

When he came up to the giant he made several strokes at him, but could not reach his body, but wounded his thighs in several places; and at length putting both hands to his sword and aiming with all his might, he cut off both his legs. Then Jack, setting his foot upon his neck, plunged his sword into the giant's body, when the monster gave a groan and expired.

The knight and his lady thanked Jack for their deliverance, and invited him to their house, to receive a proper reward for his services. "No," said Jack, "I cannot be easy till I find out this monster's habitation." So taking the knight's directions, he mounted his horse, and soon after came in sight of another giant, who was sitting on a block of timber waiting for his brother's return.

Jack alighted from his horse, and, putting on his invisible coat, approached and aimed a blow at the giant's head, but missing his aim he only cut off his nose. On this the giant seized his club and laid about him most unmercifully.

"Nay," said Jack, "if this be the case I'd better dispatch you!" so jumping upon the block, he stabbed him in the back, when he dropped down dead.

Jack then proceeded on his journey, and traveled over hills and dales, till arriving at the foot of a high mountain he knocked at the door of a lonely house, when an old man let him in.

When Jack was seated the hermit thus addressed him: "My son, on the top of this mountain is an enchanted castle, kept by the giant Galligantus and a vile magician. I lament the fate of a duke's daughter, whom they seized as she was walking in her father's garden, and brought hither transformed into a deer."

Jack promised that in the morning, at the risk of his life, he would break the enchantment; and after a sound sleep he rose early, put on his invisible coat, and got ready for the attempt.

When he had climbed to the top of the mountain he saw two fiery griffins; but he passed between them without the least fear of danger, for they could not see him because of his invisible coat. On the castle gate he found a golden trumpet, under which were written these lines:—

Whoever can this trumpet blow
Shall cause the giant's overthrow.

As soon as Jack had read this he seized the trumpet and blew a shrill blast, which made the gates fly open and the very castle itself tremble.

The giant and the conjurer now knew that their wicked course was at an end, and they stood biting their thumbs and shaking with fear. Jack, with his sword of sharpness, soon killed the giant, and the magician was then carried away by a whirlwind; and every knight and beautiful lady who had been changed into birds and beasts returned to their proper shapes. The castle vanished away like smoke, and the head of the giant Galligantus was then sent to King Arthur.

The knights and ladies rested that night at the old man's hermitage, and next day they set out for the Court. Jack then went up to the King, and gave his Majesty an account of all his fierce battles.

Jack's fame had now spread through the whole country, and at the King's desire the duke gave him his daughter in marriage, to the joy of all his kingdom. After this the King gave him a large estate, on which he and his lady lived the rest of their days in joy and contentment.

East of the Sun &
West of the Moon

O NCE UPON A TIME there was a poor husbandman who had many children and little to give them in the way either of food or clothing. They were all pretty, but the prettiest of all was the youngest daughter, who was so beautiful that there were no bounds to her beauty.

So once—it was late on a Thursday evening in autumn, and wild weather outside, terribly dark, and raining so heavily and blowing so hard that the walls of the cottage shook again—they were all sitting together by the fireside, each of them busy with something or other, when suddenly some one rapped three times against the windowpane. The man went out to see what could be the matter, and when he got out there stood a great big white bear.

"Good evening to you," said the White Bear.

"Good evening," said the man.

"Will you give me your youngest daughter?" said the White Bear; "if you will, you shall be as rich as you are now poor."

Truly the man would have had no objection to be rich, but he thought to himself: "I must first ask my daughter about this," so he went in and told them that there was a great white bear outside who had faithfully promised to make them all rich if he might but have the youngest daughter.

She said no, and would not hear of it; so the man went out again, and settled with the White Bear that he should come again next Thursday evening, and get her answer. Then the man persuaded her, and talked so much to her about the wealth that they would have, and what a good thing it would be for herself, that at last she made up her mind to go, and washed and mended all her rags, made herself as smart as she could, and held herself in readiness to set out. Little enough had she to take away with her.

Next Thursday evening the White Bear came to fetch her. She seated herself on his back with her bundle, and thus they departed.

When they had gone a great part of the way, the White Bear said: "Are you afraid?"

"No, that I am not," said she.

"Keep tight hold of my fur, and then there is no danger," said he.

And thus she rode far, far away, until they came to a great mountain. Then the White Bear knocked on it, and a door opened, and they went into a castle where there were many brilliantly lighted rooms which shone with gold and silver, likewise a large hall in which there was a well-spread table, and it was so magnificent that it would be hard to make anyone understand how splendid it was. The White Bear gave her a silver bell, and told her that when she needed anything she had but to ring this bell, and what she wanted would appear. So after she had eaten, and night was drawing near, she grew sleepy after her journey, and thought she would like to go to bed. She rang the bell, and scarcely had she touched it before she found herself in a chamber where a bed stood ready made for her, which was as pretty as anyone could wish to sleep in. It had pillows of silk, and curtains of silk fringed with gold, and everything that was in the room was of gold or silver; but when she had lain down and put out the light a man came and lay down beside her,

and behold it was the White Bear, who cast off the form of a beast during the night. She never saw him, however, for he always came after she had put out her light, and went away before daylight appeared.

So all went well and happily for a time, but then she began to be very sad and sorrowful, for all day long she had to go about alone; and she did so wish to go home to her father and mother and brothers and sisters. Then the White Bear asked what it was that she wanted, and she told him that it was so dull there in the mountain, and that she had to go about all alone, and that in her parents' house at home there were all her brothers and sisters, and it was because she could not go to them that she was so sorrowful.

"There might be a cure for that," said the White Bear, "if you would but promise me never to talk with your mother alone, but only when the others are there too; for she will take hold of your hand," he said, "and will want to lead you into a room to talk with you alone; but that you must by no means do, or you will bring great misery on both of us."

So one Sunday the White Bear came and said that they could now set out to see her father and mother, and they journeyed thither, she sitting on his back, and they went a long, long way, and it took a long, long time; but at last they came to a large white farmhouse, and her brothers and sisters were running about outside it, playing, and it was so pretty that it was a pleasure to look at it.

"Your parents dwell here now," said the White Bear; "but do not forget what I said to you, or you will do much harm both to yourself and me."

"No indeed," said she, "I shall never forget"; and as soon as she was at home the White Bear turned around and went back again.

There were such rejoicings when she went in to her parents that it seemed as if they would never come to an end. Everyone thought that he could never be sufficiently grateful to her for all she had done for them all. Now they had everything that they wanted, and everything was as good as it could be. They all asked her how she was getting on where she was. All was well with her too, she said; and she had everything that she could want. What other answers she gave I cannot say, but I am pretty sure that they did not learn much from her. But in the afternoon, after they had dined at midday, all happened just as the White Bear had said. Her mother wanted to talk with her alone in her own chamber. But she remembered what the White Bear had said, and would on no account go. "What we have to say can be said at any time," she answered. But somehow or other her mother at last persuaded her, and she was forced to tell the whole story. So she told how every night a man came and lay down beside her when the lights were all put out, and how she never saw him, because he always went away before it grew light in the morning, and how she continually went about in sadness, thinking how happy she would be if she could but see him, and how all day long she had to go about alone, and it was so dull and solitary. "Oh!" cried the mother, in horror, "you're very likely sleeping with a troll! But I will teach you a way to see him. You shall have a bit of one of my candles, which you can take away with you hidden in your breast. Look at him with that when he is asleep, but take care not to let any tallow drop upon him."

So she took the candle, and hid it in her breast, and when evening drew near the White Bear came to fetch her away. When they had gone some distance on their way, the White Bear asked her if everything had not happened just as he had foretold, and she could not but own that it had. "Then, if you have done what your mother wished," said he, "you have brought great misery on both of us." "No," she said, "I have not done anything at all." So when she had reached home and had gone to bed it was just the same as it had been before, and a man came and lay down beside her, and late at night, when she could hear that he was sleeping, she got up and kindled a light, lit her candle, let her light shine on him, and saw him, and he was the handsomest prince that eyes had ever beheld, and she loved him so much that it seemed to her that she must die if she did not kiss him that very moment. So she did kiss him; but while she was doing it she let three drops of hot tallow fall upon his shirt, and he awoke. "What have you done now?" said he; "you have brought misery on both of us. If you had but held out for the space of one year I should have been free. I have a stepmother who has bewitched me so that I am a white bear by day and a man by night; but now all is at an end between you and me, and I must leave you, and go to her. She lives in a castle which lies east of the sun and west of the moon, and there too is a princess with a nose which is three ells long, and she now is the one whom I must marry."

She wept and lamented, but all in vain, for go he must. Then she asked him if she could not go with him. But no, that could not be. "Can you tell me the way then, and I will seek you—that I may surely be allowed to do!"

"Yes, you may do that," said he; "but there is no way thither. It lies east of the sun and west of the moon, and never would you find your way there."

When she awoke in the morning both the Prince and the castle were gone, and she was lying on a small green patch in the midst of a dark, thick wood. By her side lay the self-same bundle of rags which she had brought with her from her own home. So when she had rubbed the sleep out of her eyes, and wept till she was weary, she set out on her way, and thus she walked for many and many a long day, until at last she came to a great mountain. Outside it an aged woman was sitting, playing with a golden apple. The girl asked her if she knew the way to the Prince who lived with his stepmother in the castle which lay east of the sun and west of the moon, and who was to marry a princess with a nose which was three ells long. "How do you happen to know about him?" enquired the old woman; "maybe you are she who ought to have had him." "Yes, indeed, I am," she said. "So it is you, then?" said the old woman; "I know nothing about him but that he dwells in a castle which is east of the sun and west of the moon. You will be a long time in getting to it, if ever you get to it at all; but you shall have the loan of my horse, and then you can ride on it to an old woman who is a neighbor of mine: perhaps she can tell you about him. When you have got there you must just strike the horse beneath the left ear and bid it go home again; but you may take the golden apple with you."

So the girl seated herself on the horse, and rode for a long, long way, and at last she came to the mountain, where an aged woman was sitting outside with a gold carding-comb. The girl asked her if she knew the way to the castle which lay east of the sun and west of the moon; but she said what the first old woman had said: "I know nothing about it, but that it is east of the sun and west of the moon, and that you will be a long time in getting to it, if ever you get there at all; but you shall have the loan of my horse to an old woman who lives the nearest to me: perhaps she may know where the castle is, and when you have got to her you may just strike the horse beneath the left ear and bid it go home again." Then she gave her the gold carding-comb, for it might, perhaps, be of use to her, she said.

So the girl seated herself on the horse, and rode a wearisome long way onward again, and after a very long time she came to a great mountain, where an aged woman was sitting, spinning at a golden spinning wheel. Of this woman, too, she enquired if she knew the way to the Prince, and where to find the castle which lay east of the sun and west of the moon. But it was only the same thing once again. "Maybe it was you who should have had the Prince," said the old woman. "Yes, indeed, I should have been the one," said the girl. But this old crone knew the way no better than the others—it was east of the sun and west of the moon, she knew that, "and you will be a long time in getting to it, if ever you get to it at all," she said; "but you may have the loan of my horse, and I think you had better ride to the East Wind, and ask him: perhaps he may know where the castle is, and will blow you thither. But when you have got to him you must just strike the horse beneath the left ear, and he will come home again." And then she gave her the golden spinning wheel, saying: "Perhaps you may find that you have a use for it."

The girl had to ride for a great many days, and for a long and wearisome time, before she got there; but at last she did arrive, and then she asked the East Wind if he could tell her the way to the Prince who dwelt east of the sun and west of the moon. "Well," said the East Wind, "I have heard tell of the Prince, and of his castle, but I do not know the way to it, for I have never blown so far; but, if you like, I will go with you to my brother the West Wind: he may know that, for he is much stronger than I am. You may sit on my back, and then I can carry you there." So she seated herself on his back, and they did go so swiftly! When they got there, the East Wind went in and said that the girl whom he had brought was the one who ought to have had the Prince up at the castle which lay east of the sun and west of the moon, and that now she was traveling about to find him again, so he had come there with her, and would like to hear if the West Wind knew where-abouts the castle was. "No," said the West Wind; "so far as that have I never blown: but if you like I will go with you to the South Wind, for he is much stronger than either of us, and he has roamed far and wide, and perhaps he can tell you what you want to know. You may seat yourself on my back, and then I will carry you to him."

So she did this, and journeyed to the South Wind, neither was she very long on the way. When they had got there, the West Wind asked him if he could tell her the way to the castle that lay east of the sun and west of the moon, for she was the girl who ought to marry the Prince who lived there. "Oh, indeed!" said the South Wind, "is that she? Well," said he, "I have wandered about a great deal in my time, and in all kinds of places, but I have never blown so far as that. If you like, however, I will go with you to my brother the North Wind; he is the oldest and strongest of all of us, and if he does not know where it is no one in the whole world will be able to tell you. You may sit upon my back, and then I will carry you there." So she seated herself on his back, and off he went from his house in great haste, and they were not long on the way. When they came near the North Wind's dwelling, he was so wild and frantic that they felt cold gusts a long while before they got there. "What do you want?" he roared out from afar, and they froze as they heard. Said the South Wind: "It is I, and this is she who should have had the Prince who lives in the castle which lies east of the sun and west of the moon. And now she wishes to ask you if you have ever been there, and can tell her the way, for she would gladly find him again."

"Yes," said the North Wind, "I know where it is. I once blew an aspen leaf there, but I was so tired that for many days afterward I was not able to blow at all. However, if you really are anxious to go there, and are not afraid to go with me, I will take you on my back, and try if I can blow you there."

"Get there I must," said she; "and if there is any way of going I will; and I have no fear, no matter how fast you go."

"Very well then," said the North Wind; "but you must sleep here tonight, for if we are ever to get there we must have the day before us."

The North Wind woke her betimes next morning, and puffed himself up, and made himself so big and so strong that it was frightful to see him, and away they went, high up through the air, as if they would not stop until they had reached the very end of the world. Down below there was such a storm! It blew down woods and houses, and when they were above the sea the ships were wrecked by hundreds. And thus they tore on and on, and a long time went by, and then yet more time passed, and still they were above the sea, and the North Wind grew tired, and more tired, and at last so utterly weary that he was scarcely able to blow any longer, and he sank and sank, lower and lower, until at last he went so low that the crests of the waves dashed against the heels of the poor girl he was carrying. "Art thou afraid?" said the North Wind. "I have no fear," said she; and it was true. But they were not very, very far from land, and there was just enough strength left in the

North Wind to enable him to throw her on to the shore, immediately under the windows of a castle which lay east of the sun and west of the moon; but then he was so weary and worn out that he was forced to rest for several days before he could go to his own home again.

Next morning she sat down beneath the walls of the castle to play with the golden apple, and the first person she saw was the maiden with the long nose, who was to have the Prince. "How much do you want for that gold apple of yours, girl?" said she, opening the window. "It can't be bought either for gold or money," answered the girl. "If it cannot be bought either for gold or money, what will buy it? You may say what you please," said the Princess.

"Well, if I may go to the Prince who is here, and be with him to-night, you shall have it," said the girl who had come with the North Wind. "You may do that," said the Princess, for she had made up her mind what she would do. So the Princess got the golden apple, but when the girl went up to the Prince's apartment that night he was asleep, for the Princess had so contrived it. The poor girl called to him, and shook him, and between whiles she wept; but she could not wake him. In the morning, as soon as day dawned, in came the Princess with the long nose, and drove her out again. In the daytime she sat down once more beneath the windows of the castle, and began to card with her golden carding-comb; and then all happened as it had happened before. The Princess asked her what she wanted for it, and she replied that it was not for sale, either for gold or money, but that if she could get leave to go to the Prince, and be with him during the night, she should have it. But when she went up to the Prince's room he was again asleep, and, let her call him, or shake him, or weep as she would, he still slept on, and she could not put any life in him. When daylight came in the morning, the Princess with the long nose came too, and

once more drove her away. When day had quite come, the girl seated herself under the castle windows, to spin with her golden spinning wheel, and the Princess with the long nose wanted to have that also. So she opened the window, and asked what she would take for it. The girl said what she had said on each of the former occasions—that it was not for sale either for gold or for money, but if she could get leave to go to the Prince who lived there, and be with him during the night, she should have it. "Yes," said the Princess, "I will gladly consent to that."

But in that place there were some Christian folk who had been carried off, and they had been sitting in the chamber which was next to that of the Prince, and had heard how a woman had been in there who had wept and called on him two nights running, and they told the Prince of this. So that evening, when the Princess came once more with her sleeping-drink, he pretended to drink, but threw it away behind him, for he suspected that it was a sleeping-drink. So, when the girl went into the Prince's room this time he was awake, and she had to tell him how she had come there. "You have come just in time," said the Prince, "for I should have been married tomorrow; but I will not have the long-nosed Princess, and you alone can save me. I will say that I want to see what my bride can do, and bid her wash the shirt which has the three drops of tallow on it. This she will consent to do, for she does not know that it is you who let them fall on it; but no one can wash them out but one born of Christian folk: it cannot be done by one of a pack of trolls; and then I will say that no one shall ever be my bride but the woman who can do this, and I know that you can." There was great joy and gladness between them all that night, but the next day, when the wedding was to take place, the Prince said, "I must see what my bride can do." "That you may do," said the stepmother.

"I have a fine shirt which I want to wear as my wedding shirt, but three drops of tallow have got upon it which I want to have washed off, and I have vowed to marry no one but the woman who is able to do it. If she cannot do that, she is not worth having."

Well, that was a very small matter, they thought, and agreed to do it. The Princess with the long nose began to wash as well as she could, but, the more she washed and rubbed, the larger the spots grew. "Ah! you can't wash at all," said the old troll-hag, who was her mother. "Give it to me." But she too had not had the shirt very long in her hands before it looked worse still, and, the more she washed it and rubbed it, the larger and blacker grew the spots.

So the other trolls had to come and wash, but, the more they did, the blacker and uglier grew the shirt, until at length it was as black as if it had been up the chimney. "Oh," cried the Prince, "not one of you is good for anything at all. There is a beggar-girl sitting outside the window, and I'll be bound that she can wash better than any of you! Come in, you girl there!" he cried. So she came in. "Can you wash this shirt clean?" he cried. "Oh! I don't know," she said; "but I will try." And no sooner had she taken the shirt and dipped it in the water than it was white as driven snow, and even whiter than that. "I will marry you," said the Prince.

Then the old troll-hag flew into such a rage that she burst, and the Princess with the long nose and all the little trolls must have burst too, for they have never been heard of since. The Prince and his bride set free all the Christian folk who were imprisoned there, and took away with them all the gold and silver that they could carry, and moved far away from the castle which lay east of the sun and west of the moon.

Hansel and Grettel

ONCE UPON A TIME there dwelt on the outskirts of a large forest a poor woodcutter with his wife and two children; the boy was called Hansel and the girl Grettel. He had always little enough to live on, and once, when there was a great famine in the land, he couldn't even provide them with daily bread. One night, as he was tossing about in bed, full of cares and worry, he sighed and said to his wife: "What's to become of us? How are we to support our poor children, now that we have nothing more for ourselves?" "I'll tell you what, husband," answered the woman; "early tomorrow morning we'll take the children out into the thickest part of the wood; there we shall light a fire for them and give them each a piece of bread; then we'll go on to our work and leave them alone. They won't be able to find their way home, and we shall thus be rid of them." "No, wife," said her husband, "that I won't do; how could I find it in my heart to leave my children alone in the wood? The wild beasts would soon come and tear them to pieces." "Oh! you fool," said she, "then we must all four die of hunger, and you may just as well go and plane the boards for our coffins"; and she left him no peace till he consented. "But I can't help feeling sorry for the poor children," added the husband.

The children, too, had not been able to sleep for hunger, and had heard what their stepmother had said to their father. Grettel wept bitterly and spoke to Hansel: "Now it's all up with us." "No, no,

93

Grettel," said Hansel, "don't fret yourself; I'll be able to find a way of escape, no fear." And when the old people had fallen asleep he got up, slipped on his little coat, opened the back door and stole out. The moon was shining clearly, and the white pebbles which lay in front of the house glittered like bits of silver. Hansel bent down and filled his pocket with as many of them as he could cram in. Then he went back and said to Grettel: "Be comforted, my dear little sister, and go to sleep: God will not desert us"; and he lay down in bed again.

At daybreak, even before the sun was up, the woman came and woke the two children: "Get up, you lie-abeds, we're all going to the forest to fetch wood." She gave them each a bit of bread and spoke: "There's something for your luncheon, but don't you eat it up before, for it's all you'll get." Grettel took the bread under her apron, as Hansel had the stones in his pocket. Then they all set out together on the way to the forest. After they had walked for a little, Hansel stood still and looked back at the house, and this maneuver he repeated again and again. His father observed him, and spake: "Hansel, what are you gazing at there, and why do you always remain behind? Take care, and don't lose your footing." "Oh! father," said Hansel, "I am looking back at my white kitten, which is sitting on the roof, waving me a farewell." The woman exclaimed: "What a donkey you are! That isn't your kitten, that's the morning sun shining on the chimney." But Hansel had not looked back at his kitten, but had always dropped one of the white pebbles out of his pocket on to the path.

When they had reached the middle of the forest the father said: "Now, children, go and fetch a lot of wood, and I'll light a fire that you mayn't feel cold." Hansel and Grettel heaped up brushwood till they had made a pile nearly the size of a small hill. The brushwood was set fire to, and when the flames leaped high the woman said: "Now lie down at the fire, children, and rest yourselves: we are going into the forest to cut down wood; when we've finished we'll come back and fetch you." Hansel and Grettel sat down beside the fire, and at midday ate their little bits of bread. They heard the strokes of the axe, so they thought their father was quite near. But it was no axe they heard, but a bough he had tied on to a dead tree, and that was blown about by the wind. And when they had sat for a long time their eyes closed with fatigue, and they fell fast asleep. When they awoke at last it was pitch-dark. Grettel began to cry, and said: "How are we ever to get out of the wood?" But Hansel comforted her. "Wait a bit," he said, "till the moon is up, and then we'll find our way sure enough." And when the full moon had risen he took his sister by the hand and followed the pebbles, which shone like new threepenny bits, and showed them the path. They walked all through the night, and at daybreak reached their father's house again. They knocked at the door, and when the woman opened it she exclaimed: "You naughty children, what a time you've slept in the wood! We thought you were never going to come back." But the father rejoiced, for his conscience had reproached him for leaving his children behind by themselves.

Not long afterward there was again great dearth in the land, and the children heard their mother address their father thus in bed one night: "Everything is eaten up once more; we have only half a loaf in the house, and when that's done it's all up with us. The children must be got rid of; we'll lead them deeper into the wood this time, so that they won't be able to find their way out again. There is no other way of saving ourselves." The man's heart smote him heavily, and he thought: "Surely it would be better to share the last bite with one's children!" But his wife wouldn't listen to his arguments, and did nothing but scold and reproach him. If a man yields once he's done for, and so, because he had given in the first time, he was forced to do so the second.

But the children were awake, and had heard the conversation.

Hansel and Grettel

When the old people were asleep Hansel got up, and wanted to go out and pick up pebbles again, as he had done the first time; but the woman had barred the door, and Hansel couldn't get out. But he consoled his little sister, and said: "Don't cry, Grettel, and sleep peacefully, for God is sure to help us."

At early dawn the woman came and made the children get up. They received their bit of bread, but it was even smaller than the time before. On the way to the wood Hansel crumbled it in his pocket, and every few minutes he stood still and dropped a crumb on the ground. "Hansel, what are you stopping and looking about you for?" said the father. "I'm looking back at my little pigeon, which is sitting on the roof waving me a farewell," answered Hansel. "Fool!" said the wife; "that isn't your pigeon, it's the morning sun glittering on the chimney." But Hansel gradually threw all his crumbs on to the path. The woman led the children still deeper into the forest, farther than they had ever been in their lives before. Then a big fire was lit again, and the mother said: "Just sit down there, children, and if you're tired you can sleep a bit; we're going into the forest to cut down wood, and in the evening when we're finished we'll come back to fetch you." At midday Grettel divided her bread with Hansel, for he had strewed his all along their path. Then they fell asleep, and evening passed away, but nobody came to the poor children. They didn't awake till it was pitch-dark, and Hansel comforted his sister, saying: "Only wait, Grettel, till the moon rises, then we shall see the bread-crumbs I scattered along the path; they will show us the way back to the house." When the moon appeared they got up, but they found no crumbs, for the thousands of birds that fly about the woods and fields had picked them all up. "Never mind," said Hansel to Grettel; "you'll see we'll still find a way out"; but all the same they did not. They wandered about the whole night, and the next day, from morning till evening, but they could not find a path out of the wood. They were very hungry, too, for they had nothing to eat but a few berries they found growing on the ground. And at last they were so tired that their legs refused to carry them any longer, so they lay down under a tree and fell fast asleep.

On the third morning after they had left their father's house they set about their wandering again, but only got deeper and deeper into the wood, and now they felt that if help did not come to them soon they must perish. At midday they saw a beautiful little snow-white bird sitting on a branch, which sang so sweetly that they stopped still and listened to it. And when its song was finished it flapped its wings and flew on in front of them. They followed it and came to a little house, on the roof of which it perched; and when they came quite near they saw that the cottage was made of bread and roofed with cakes, while the window was made of transparent sugar. "Now we'll set to," said Hansel, "and have a regular blow-out. I'll eat a bit of the roof, and you, Grettel, can eat some of the window, which you'll find a sweet morsel." Hansel stretched up his hand and broke off a little bit of the roof to see what it was like, and Grettel went to the casement and began to nibble at it. Thereupon a shrill voice called out from the room inside:

"Nibble, nibble, little mouse.
Who's nibbling my house?"

The children answered:

"'Tis Heaven's own child,
The tempest wild,"

and went on eating, without putting themselves about. Hansel, who thoroughly appreciated the roof, tore down a big bit of it, while Grettel pushed out a whole round windowpane, and sat down the better to enjoy it. Suddenly the door opened, and an ancient dame leaning on a staff hobbled out. Hansel and Grettel were so terrified that they let what they had in their hands fall. But the old woman shook her head and said: "Oh, ho! you dear children, who led you here? Just come in and stay with me, no ill shall befall you." She took them both by the hand and led them into the house, and laid a most sumptuous dinner before them—milk and sugared pancakes, with apples and nuts. After they had finished, two beautiful little white beds were prepared for them, and when Hansel and Grettel lay down in them they felt as if they had got into heaven.

The old woman had appeared to be most friendly, but she was really an old witch who had waylaid the children, and had only built the little bread house in order to lure them in. When anyone came into her power she killed, cooked, and ate him, and held a regular feast-day for the occasion. Now witches have red eyes, and cannot see far, but, like beasts, they have a keen sense of smell, and know when human beings pass by. When Hansel and Grettel fell into her hands she laughed maliciously, and said jeeringly: "I've got them now; they shan't escape me." Early in the morning, before the children were awake, she rose up, and when she saw them both sleeping so peacefully, with their round rosy cheeks, she muttered to herself: "That'll be a dainty bite." Then she seized Hansel with her bony hand and carried him into a little stable, and barred the door on him; he might scream as much as he liked, it did him no good. Then she went to Grettel, shook her till she awoke, and cried: "Get up, you lazy-bones, fetch water and cook something for your brother. When he's fat I'll eat him up." Grettel began to cry bitterly, but it was of no use: she had to do what the wicked witch bade her.

Hansel and Grettel

So the best food was cooked for poor Hansel, but Grettel got nothing but crab-shells. Every morning the old woman hobbled out to the stable and cried: "Hansel, put out your finger, that I may feel if you are getting fat." But Hansel always stretched out a bone, and the old dame, whose eyes were dim, couldn't see it, and thinking always it was Hansel's finger, wondered why he fattened so slowly. When four weeks passed and Hansel still remained thin, she lost patience and determined to wait no longer. "Hi! Grettel," she called to the girl, "be quick and get some water. Hansel may be fat or thin, I'm going to kill him tomorrow and cook him." Oh! how the poor little sister sobbed as she carried the water, and how the tears rolled down her cheeks! "Kind heaven help us now!" she cried; "if only the wild beasts in the wood had eaten us, then at least we should have died together." "Just hold your peace," said the old hag; "it won't help you."

Early in the morning Grettel had to go out and hang up the kettle full of water, and light the fire. "First we'll bake," said the old dame; "I've heated the oven already and kneaded the dough." She pushed Grettel out to the oven, from which fiery flames were already issuing. "Creep in," said the witch, "and see if it's properly heated, so that we can shove in the bread." For when she had got Grettel in she meant to close the oven and let the girl bake, that she might eat her up too. But Grettel perceived her intention, and spoke: "I don't know how I'm to do it; how do I get in?" "You silly goose!" said the hag, "the opening is big enough; see, I could get in myself;" and she crawled toward it, and poked her head into the oven. Then Grettel gave her a shove that sent her right in, shut the iron door, and drew the bolt. Gracious! how she yelled! it was quite horrible; but Grettel fled, and the wretched old woman was left to perish miserably.

Grettel flew straight to Hansel, opened the little stable door, and cried: "Hansel, we are free; the old witch is dead." Then Hansel sprang like a bird out of a cage when the door is opened. How they rejoiced, and fell on each other's necks, and jumped for joy, and kissed one another! And as they had no longer any cause for fear, they went into the old hag's house, and there they found, in every corner of the room, boxes with pearls and precious stones. "These are even better than pebbles," said Hansel, and crammed his pockets full of them; and Grettel said: "I too will bring something home"; and she filled her apron full. "But now," said Hansel, "let's go and get well away from the witches' wood." When they had wandered about for some hours they came to a big lake. "We can't get over," said Hansel; "I see no bridge of any sort or kind." "Yes, and there's no ferryboat either," answered Grettel; "but look, there swims a white duck; if I ask her she'll help us over"; and she called out:

Hansel and Grettel

"Here are two children, mournful very,
Seeing neither bridge nor ferry;
Take us upon your white back,
And row us over, quack, quack!"

The duck swam toward them, and Hansel got on her back and bade his little sister sit beside him. "No," answered Grettel, "we should be too heavy a load for the duck: she shall carry us across separately." The good bird did this, and when they were landed safely on the other side, and had gone on for a while, the wood became more and more familiar to them, and at length they saw their father's house in the distance. Then they set off to run, and bounding into the room fell on their father's neck. The man had not passed a happy hour since he left them in the wood, but the woman had died. Grettel shook out her apron so that the pearls and precious stones rolled about the room, and Hansel threw down one handful after the other out of his pocket. Thus all their troubles were ended, and they all lived happily ever afterward.

My story is done. See! there runs a little mouse; anyone who catches it may make himself a large fur cap out of it.

The Snake Prince

❦

ONCE UPON A TIME there lived by herself, in a city, an old woman who was desperately poor. One day she found that she had only a handful of flour left in the house, and no money to buy more nor hope of earning it. Carrying her little brass pot, very sadly she made her way down to the river to bathe and to obtain some water, thinking afterward to come home and make herself an unleavened cake of what flour she had left; and after that she did not know what was to become of her.

Whilst she was bathing she left her little brass pot on the river bank covered with a cloth, to keep the inside nice and clean; but when she came up out of the river and took the cloth off to fill the pot with water, she saw inside it the glittering folds of a deadly snake. At once she popped the cloth again into the mouth of the pot and held it there; and then she said to herself:

"Ah, kind death! I will take thee home to my house, and there I will shake thee out of my pot and thou shalt bite me and I will die, and then all my troubles will be ended."

With these sad thoughts in her mind the poor old woman hurried home, holding her cloth carefully in the mouth of the pot; and when she got home she shut all the doors and windows, and took away the cloth, and turned the pot upside down upon her hearthstone. What was her surprise to find that, instead of the deadly snake which she expected to see fall out of it, there fell out with a rattle and a clang a most magnificent necklace of flashing jewels!

For a few minutes she could hardly think or speak, but stood staring; and then with trembling hands she picked the necklace up, and folding it in the corner of her veil, she hurried off to the king's hall of public audience.

"A petition, O king!" she said. "A petition for thy private ear alone!" And when her prayer had been granted, and she found herself alone with the king, she shook out her veil at his feet, and there fell from it in glittering coils the splendid necklace. As soon as the king saw it he was filled with amazement and delight; and the more he looked at it the more he felt that he must possess it at once. So he gave the old woman five hundred silver pieces for it, and put it straightway into his pocket. Away she went full of happiness; for the money that the king had given her was enough to keep her for the rest of her life.

As soon as he could leave his business the king hurried off and showed his wife his prize, with which she was as pleased as he, if not more so; and, as soon as they had finished admiring the wonderful necklace, they locked it up in the great chest where the queen's jewelry was kept, the key of which hung always around the king's neck.

A short while afterward, a neighboring king sent a message to say that a most lovely girl baby had been born to him; and he invited his neighbors to come to a great feast in honor of the occasion. The queen told her husband that of course they must be present at the banquet, and she would wear the new necklace which he had given her. They had only a short time to prepare for the journey, and at the last moment the king went to the jewel chest to take out the necklace for his wife to wear, but he could see no necklace at all, only, in its place, a fat little boy baby crowing and shouting. The king was so astonished that he nearly fell backward, but presently he found his voice, and called for his wife so loudly that she came running, thinking that the necklace must at least have been stolen.

"Look here! look!" cried the king, "haven't we always longed for a son? And now heaven has sent us one!"

"What do you mean?" cried the queen. "Are you mad?"

"Mad? no, I hope not," shouted the king, dancing in excitement around the open chest. "Come here, and look! Look what we've got instead of that necklace!"

Just then the baby let out a great crow of joy, as though he would like to jump up and dance with the king; and the queen gave a cry of surprise, and ran up and looked into the chest.

"Oh!" she gasped, as she looked at the baby, "what a darling! Where could he have come from?"

"I'm sure I can't say," said the king; "all I know is that we locked up a necklace in the chest, and when I unlocked it just now there was no necklace, but a baby, and as fine a baby as ever was seen."

By this time the queen had the baby in her arms. "Oh, the blessed one!" she cried, "fairer ornament for the bosom of a queen than any necklace that ever was wrought. Write," she continued, "write to our neighbor and say that we cannot come to his feast, for we have a feast of our own, and a baby of our own! Oh, happy day!"

So the visit was given up; and, in honor of the new baby, the bells of the city, and its guns, and its trumpets, and its people, small and great, had hardly any rest for a week; there was such a ringing, and banging, and blaring, and such fireworks, and feasting, and rejoicing, and merry-making, as had never been seen before.

A few years went by; and, as the king's boy baby and his neighbor's girl baby grew and throve, the two kings arranged that as soon as they were old enough they should marry; and so, with much signing of papers and agreements, and wagging of wise heads, and stroking of gray beards, the compact was made, and signed, and sealed, and lay waiting, for its fulfillment. And this too came to pass; for, as soon as the prince and princess were eighteen years of age, the kings agreed that it was time for the wedding; and the young prince journeyed away to the neighboring kingdom for his bride, and was there married to her with great and renewed rejoicings.

Now, I must tell you that the old woman who had sold the king the necklace had been called in by him to be the nurse of the young prince; and although she loved her charge dearly, and was a most faithful servant, she could not help talking just a little, and so, by and by, it began to be rumored that there was some magic about the young prince's birth; and the rumor of course had come in due time to the ears of the parents of the princess. So now that she was going to be the wife of the prince, her mother (who was curious, as many other people are) said to her daughter on the eve of the ceremony:

"Remember that the first thing you must do is to find out what this story is about the prince. And, in order to do it, you must not speak a word to him whatever he says until he asks you why you are silent; then you must ask him what the truth is about his magic birth; and until he tells you, you must not speak to him again."

And the princess promised that she would follow her mother's advice.

Therefore when they were married, and the prince spoke to his bride, she did not answer him. He could not think what was the matter, but even about her old home she would not utter a word. At last he asked why she would not speak; and then she said:

"Tell me the secret of your birth."

Then the prince was very sad and displeased, and although she pressed him sorely he would not tell her, but always reply:

"If I tell you, you will repent that ever you asked me."

For several months they lived together; and it was not such a happy time for either as it ought to have been, for the secret was still a secret, and lay between them like a cloud between the sun and the earth, making what should be fair, dull and sad.

At length the prince could bear it no longer; so he said to his wife one day: "At midnight I will tell you my secret if you still wish it; but you will repent it all your life." However, the princess was overjoyed that she had succeeded, and paid no attention to his warnings.

That night the prince ordered horses to be ready for the princess and himself a little before midnight. He placed her on one, and mounted the other himself, and they rode together down to the river to the place where the old woman had first found the snake in her brass pot. There the prince drew rein and said sadly: "Do you still insist that I should tell you my secret?" And the princess answered, "Yes." "If I do," answered the prince, "remember that you will regret it all your life." But the princess only replied, "Tell me!"

"Then," said the prince, "know that I am the son of the king of a far country, but by enchantment I was turned into a snake."

The word "snake" was hardly out of his lips when he disappeared, and the princess heard a rustle and saw a ripple on the water; and in the faint moonlight she beheld a snake swimming into the river. Soon it disappeared and she was left alone. In vain she waited with beating heart for something to happen, and for the prince to come back to her. Nothing happened and no one came; only the wind mourned through the trees on the river bank, and the night birds cried, and a jackal howled in the distance, and the river flowed black and silent beneath her.

In the morning they found her, weeping and disheveled, on the river bank; but no word could they learn from her or from anyone as to the fate of her husband. At her wish they built on the river bank a little house of black stone; and there she lived in mourning, with a few servants and guards to watch over her.

A long, long time passed by, and still the princess lived in mourning for her prince, and saw no one, and went nowhere away from her house on the river bank and the garden that surrounded it. One morning, when she woke up, she found a stain of fresh mud upon the carpet. She sent for the guards, who watched outside the house day and night, and asked them who had entered her room while she was asleep. They declared that no one *could* have entered, for they kept such careful watch that not even a bird could fly in without their knowledge; but none of them could explain the stain of mud. The next morning, again, the princess found another stain of wet mud, and she questioned everyone most carefully; but none could say how the mud came there. The third night the princess determined to lie awake herself and watch; and, for fear that she might fall asleep, she cut her finger with a penknife and rubbed salt into the cut, that the pain of it might keep her from sleeping. So she lay awake, and at midnight she saw a snake come wriggling along the ground with some mud from the river in its mouth; and when it came near the bed, it reared up its head and dropped its muddy head on the bedclothes. She was very frightened, but tried to control her fear, and called out:

"Who are you, and what do you here?"

And the snake answered:

"I am the prince, your husband, and I am come to visit you."

Then the princess began to weep; and the snake continued:

"Alas! did I not say that if I told you my secret you would repent it? and have you not repented?"

"Oh, indeed!" cried the poor princess, "I have repented it, and shall repent it all my life! Is there nothing I can do?"

And the snake answered:

"Yes, there is one thing, if you dared to do it."

"Only tell me," said the princess, "and I will do *anything!*"

"Then," replied the snake, "on a certain night you must put a large bowl of milk and sugar in each of the four corners of this room. All the snakes in the river will come out to drink the milk, and the one that leads the way will be the queen of the snakes. You must stand in her way at the door, and say: 'Oh, Queen of Snakes, Queen of Snakes, give me back my husband!' and perhaps she will do it. But if you are frightened, and do not stop her, you will never see me again." And he glided away.

On the night of which the snake had told her, the princess got four large bowls of milk and sugar, and put one in each corner of the room, and stood in the doorway waiting. At midnight there was a great hissing and rustling from the direction of the river, and presently the ground appeared to be alive with horrible writhing forms of snakes, whose eyes glittered and forked tongues quivered as they moved on in the direction of the princess's house. Foremost among them was a huge, repulsive scaly creature that led the dreadful procession. The guards were so terrified that they all ran away; but the princess stood in the doorway, as white as death, and with her hands clasped tight together for fear she

should scream or faint, and fail to do her part. As they came closer and saw her in the way, all the snakes raised their horrid heads and swayed them to and fro, and looked at her with wicked beady eyes, while their breath seemed to poison the very air. Still the princess stood firm, and, when the leading snake was within a few feet of her, she cried: "Oh, Queen of Snakes, Queen of Snakes, give me back my husband!" Then all the rustling, writhing crowd of snakes seemed to whisper to one another "Her husband? her husband?" But the queen of snakes moved on until her head was almost in the princess's face, and her little eyes seemed to flash fire. And still the princess stood in the doorway and never moved, but cried again: "Oh, Queen of Snakes, Queen of Snakes, give me back my husband!" Then the queen of snakes replied: "Tomorrow you shall have him—tomorrow!" When she heard these words and knew that she had conquered, the princess staggered from the door, and sank upon her bed and fainted. As in a dream, she saw that her room was full of snakes, all jostling and squabbling over the bowls of milk until it was finished. And then they went away.

In the morning the princess was up early, and took off the mourning dress which she had worn for five whole years, and put on gay and beautiful clothes. And she swept the house and cleaned it, and adorned it with garlands and nosegays of sweet flowers and ferns, and prepared it as though she were making ready for her wedding. And when night fell she lit up the woods and gardens with lanterns, and spread a table as for a feast, and lit in the house a thousand wax candles. Then she waited for her husband, not knowing in what shape he would appear. And at midnight there came striding from the river the prince, laughing, but with tears in his eyes; and she ran to meet him, and threw herself into his arms, crying and laughing too.

So the prince came home; and the next day they two went back to the palace, and the old king wept with joy to see them. And the bells, so long silent, were set a-ringing again, and the guns firing, and the trumpets blaring, and there was fresh feasting and rejoicing.

And the old woman who had been the prince's nurse became nurse to the prince's children—at least she was called so; though she was far too old to do anything for them but love them. Yet she still thought that she was useful, and knew that she was happy. And happy, indeed, were the prince and princess, who in due time became king and queen, and lived and ruled long and prosperously.

The Three Little Pigs

❦

THERE WAS ONCE UPON A TIME a pig who lived with her three children on a large, comfortable, old-fashioned farmyard. The eldest of the little pigs was called Browny, the second Whitey, and the youngest and best looking Blacky. Now Browny was a very dirty little pig, and I am sorry to say spent most of his time rolling and wallowing about in the mud. He was never so happy as on a wet day, when the mud in the farmyard got soft, and thick, and slab. Then he would steal away from his mother's side, and finding the muddiest place in the yard, would roll about in it and thoroughly enjoy himself. His mother often found fault with him for this, and would shake her head sadly and say: "Ah, Browny! some day you will be sorry that you did not obey your old mother." But no words of advice or warning could cure Browny of his bad habits.

Whitey was quite a clever little pig, but she was greedy. She was always thinking of her food, and looking forward to her dinner; and when the farm girl was seen carrying the pails across the yard, she would rise up on her hind legs and dance and caper with excitement. As soon as the food was poured into the trough she jostled Blacky and Browny out of the way in her eagerness to get the best and biggest bits for herself. Her mother often scolded her for her selfishness, and told her that some day she would suffer for being so greedy and grabbing.

Blacky was a good, nice little pig, neither dirty nor greedy. He had nice dainty ways (for a pig), and his skin was always as smooth and shining as black satin. He was much cleverer than Browny and Whitey, and his mother's heart used to swell with pride when she heard the farmer's friends say to each other that some day the little black fellow would be a prize pig.

Now the time came when the mother pig felt old and feeble and near her end. One day she called the three little pigs around her and said:

"My children, I feel that I am growing old and weak, and that I shall not live long. Before I die I should like to build a house for each of you, as this dear old sty in which we have lived so happily will be given to a new family of pigs, and you will have to turn out. Now, Browny, what sort of a house would you like to have?"

"A house of mud," replied Browny, looking longingly at a wet puddle in the corner of the yard.

"And you, Whitey?" said the mother pig in rather a sad voice, for she was disappointed that Browny had made so foolish a choice.

"A house of cabbage," answered Whitey, with a mouth full, and scarcely raising her snout out of the trough in which she was grubbing for some potato parings.

"Foolish, foolish child!" said the mother pig, looking quite distressed. "And you, Blacky?" turning to her youngest son, "what sort of a house shall I order for you?"

"A house of brick, please mother, as it will be warm in winter, and cool in summer, and safe all the year round."

"That is a sensible little pig," replied his mother, looking fondly at him. "I will see that the three houses are got ready at once. And now one last piece of advice. You have heard me talk of our old enemy the

fox. When he hears that I am dead, he is sure to try and get hold of you, to carry you off to his den. He is very sly and will no doubt disguise himself, and pretend to be a friend, but you must promise me not to let him enter your houses on any pretext whatever."

And the little pigs readily promised, for they had always had great fear of the fox, of whom they had heard many terrible tales. A short time afterward the old pig died, and the little pigs went to live in their own houses.

Browny was quite delighted with his soft mud walls and with the clay floor, which soon looked like nothing but a big mud pie. But that was what Browny enjoyed, and he was as happy as possible, rolling about all day and making himself in such a mess. One day, as he was lying half asleep in the mud, he heard a soft knock at his door, and a gentle voice said:

"May I come in, Master Browny? I want to see your beautiful new house."

"Who are you?" said Browny, starting up in great fright, for though the voice sounded gentle, he felt sure it was a feigned voice, and he feared it was the fox.

"I am a friend come to call on you," answered the voice.

"No, no," replied Browny, "I don't believe you are a friend. You are the wicked fox, against whom our mother warned us. I won't let you in."

"Oho! is that the way you answer me?" said the fox, speaking very roughly in his natural voice. "We shall soon see who is master here," and with his paws he set to work and scraped a large hole in the soft mud walls. A moment later he had jumped through it, and catching Browny by the neck, flung him on his shoulders and trotted off with him to his den.

The next day, as Whitey was munching a few leaves of cabbage out of the corner of her house, the fox stole up to her door, determined to carry her off to join her brother in his den. He began speaking to her in the same feigned gentle voice in which he had spoken to Browny; but it frightened her very much when he said:

"I am a friend come to visit you, and to have some of your good cabbage for my dinner."

"Please don't touch it," cried Whitey in great distress. "The cabbages are the walls of my house, and if you eat them you will make a hole, and the wind and rain will come in and give me a cold. Do go away; I am sure you are not a friend, but our wicked enemy the fox." And poor Whitey began to whine and to whimper, and to wish that she had not been such a greedy little pig, and had chosen a more solid material than cabbages for her house. But it was too late now, and in another minute the fox had eaten his way through the cabbage walls, and had caught the trembling, shivering Whitey, and carried her off to his den.

The next day the fox started off for Blacky's house, because he had made up his mind that he would get the three little pigs together in his den, and then kill them, and invite all his friends to feast. But when he reached the brick house, he found that the door was bolted and barred, so in his sly manner he began, "Do let me in, dear Blacky. I have brought you a present of some eggs that I picked up in a farmyard on my way here."

"No, no, Mister Fox," replied Blacky, "I am not going to open my door to you. I know your cunning ways. You have carried off poor Browny and Whitey, but you are not going to get me."

At this the fox was so angry that he dashed with all his force against the wall, and tried to knock it down. But it was too strong and well-built; and though the fox scraped and tore at the bricks with his paws he only hurt himself, and at last he had to give it up, and limp away with his forepaws all bleeding and sore.

"Never mind!" he cried angrily as he went off. "I'll catch you another day, see if I don't, and won't I grind your bones to powder when I have got you in my den!" and he snarled fiercely and showed his teeth.

Next day Blacky had to go into the neighboring town to do some marketing and to buy a big kettle. As he was walking home with it slung over his shoulder, he heard a sound of steps stealthily creeping after him. For a moment his heart stood still with fear, and then a happy thought came to him. He had just reached the top of a hill, and could see his own little house nestling at the foot of it among the trees. In a moment he had snatched the lid off the kettle and had jumped in himself. Coiling himself round he lay quite snug in the bottom of the kettle, while with his foreleg he managed to put the lid on, so that he was entirely hidden. With a little kick from the inside he started the kettle off, and down the hill it rolled full tilt; and when the fox came up, all that he saw was a large black kettle spinning over the ground at

a great pace. Very much disappointed, he was just going to turn away, when he saw the kettle stop close to the little brick house, and in a moment later Blacky jumped out of it and escaped with the kettle into the house, when he barred and bolted the door, and put the shutter up over the window.

"Oho!" exclaimed the fox to himself, "you think you will escape me that way, do you? We shall soon see about that, my friend," and very quietly and stealthily he prowled around the house looking for some way to climb on to the roof.

In the meantime Blacky had filled the kettle with water, and having put it on the fire, sat down quietly waiting for it to boil. Just as the kettle was beginning to sing, and steam to come out of the spout, he heard a sound like a soft, muffled step, patter, patter, patter overhead, and the next moment the fox's head and forepaws were seen coming down the chimney. But Blacky very wisely had not put the lid on the kettle, and, with a yelp of pain, the fox fell into the boiling water, and before he could escape, Blacky had popped the lid on, and the fox was scalded to death.

As soon as he was sure that their wicked enemy was really dead, and could do them no further harm, Blacky started off to rescue Browny and Whitey. As he approached the den he heard piteous grunts and squeals from his poor little brother and sister who lived in constant terror of the fox killing and eating them. But when they saw Blacky appear at the entrance to the den their joy knew no bounds. He quickly found a sharp stone and cut the cords by which they were tied to a stake in the ground, and then all three started off together for Blacky's house, where they lived happily ever after; and Browny quite gave up rolling in the mud, and Whitey ceased to be greedy, and they never forgot how nearly these faults had brought them to an untimely end.

The Flying Ship

❦

ONCE UPON A TIME there lived an old couple who had three sons; the two elder were clever, but the third was a regular dunce. The clever sons were very fond of their mother, gave her good clothes, and always spoke pleasantly to her; but the youngest was always getting in her way, and she had no patience with him. Now, one day it was announced in the village that the King had issued a decree, offering his daughter, the Princess, in marriage to whomever should build a ship that could fly. Immediately the two elder brothers determined to try their luck, and asked their parents' blessing. So the old mother smartened up their clothes, and gave them a store of provisions for their journey, not forgetting to add a bottle of brandy. When they had gone the poor Simpleton began to tease his mother to smarten him up and let him start off.

"What would become of a dolt like you?" she answered. "Why, you would be eaten up by wolves."

But the foolish youth kept repeating, "I will go, I will go, I will go!"

Seeing that she could do nothing with him, the mother gave him a crust of bread and a bottle of water, and took no further heed of him.

So the Simpleton set off on his way. When he had gone a short distance he met a little old manikin. They greeted one another, and the manikin asked him where he was going.

"I am off to the King's Court," he answered. "He has promised to

The Flying Ship

give his daughter to whomever can make a flying ship."

"And can you make such a ship?"

"Not I."

"Then why in the world are you going?"

"Can't tell," replied the Simpleton.

"Well, if that is the case," said the manikin, "sit down beside me; we can rest for a little and have something to eat. Give me what you have got in your satchel."

Now, the poor Simpleton was ashamed to show what was in it. However, he thought it best not to make a fuss, so he opened the satchel, and could scarcely believe his own eyes, for, instead of the hard crust, he saw two beautiful fresh rolls and some cold meat. He shared them with the manikin, who licked his lips and said:

"Now, go into that wood, and stop in front of the first tree, bow three times, and then strike the tree with your axe, fall on your knees on the ground, with your face on the earth, and remain there till you are raised up. You will then find a ship at your side, step into it and fly to the King's Palace. If you meet anyone on the way, take him with you."

The Simpleton thanked the manikin very kindly, bade him farewell, and went into the road. When he got to the first tree he stopped in front of it, did everything just as he had been told, and, kneeling on the ground with his face to the earth, fell asleep. After a little time he was aroused; he awoke and, rubbing his eyes, saw a ready-made ship at his side, and at once got into it. And the ship rose and rose, and in another minute was flying through the air, when the Simpleton, who was on the look-out, cast his eyes down to the earth and saw a man beneath him on the road, who was kneeling with his ear upon the damp ground.

"Hallo!" he called out, "what are you doing down there?"

"I am listening to what is going on in the world," replied the man.

"Come with me in my ship," said the Simpleton.

So the man was only too glad, and got in beside him; and the ship flew, and flew, and flew through the air, till again from his outlook the Simpleton saw a man on the road below, who was hopping on one leg, while his other leg was tied up behind his ear. So he hailed him, calling out:

"Hallo! what are you doing hopping on one leg?"

"I can't help it," replied the man. "I walk so fast that unless I tied up one leg I should be at the end of the earth in a bound."

"Come with us on my ship," he answered; and the man made no objections, but joined them; and the ship flew on, and on, and on, till suddenly the Simpleton, looking down on the road below, beheld a man aiming with a gun into the distance.

"Hallo!" he shouted to him, "what are you aiming at? As far as eye can see, there is no bird in sight."

"What would be the good of my taking a near shot?" replied the man. "I can hit beast or bird at a hundred miles' distance. That is the kind of shot I enjoy."

"Come into the ship with us," answered the Simpleton; and the man was only too glad to join them, and he got in; and the ship flew on, farther and farther, till again the Simpleton from his outlook saw a man on the road below, carrying on his back a basket full of bread. And he waved to him, calling out:

"Hallo! where are you going?"

"To fetch bread for my breakfast."

"Bread? Why, you have got a whole basket-load of it on your back."

"That's nothing," answered the man; "I should finish that in one mouthful."

"Come along with us in my ship, then."

And so the glutton joined the party, and the ship mounted again into the air, and flew up and onward, till the Simpleton from his outlook saw a man walking by the shore of a great lake, and evidently looking for something.

"Hallo!" he cried to him, "what are you seeking?"

"I want water to drink, I'm so thirsty," replied the man.

"Well, there's a whole lake in front of you; why don't you drink some of that?"

"Do you call that enough?" answered the other. "Why, I should drink it up in one gulp."

"Well, come with us in the ship."

And so the mighty drinker was added to the company; and the ship flew farther, and even farther, till again the Simpleton looked out, and this time he saw a man dragging a bundle of wood, walking through the forest beneath them.

"Hallo!" he shouted to him, "why are you carrying wood through a forest?"

"This is not common wood," answered the other.

"What sort of wood is it, then?" said the Simpleton.

"If you throw it upon the ground," said the man, "it will be changed into an army of soldiers."

"Come into the ship with us, then."

And so he too joined them; and away the ship flew on, and on, and on, and once more the Simpleton looked out, and this time he saw a man carrying straw upon his back.

"Hallo! where are you carrying that straw to?"

"To the village," said the man.

"Do you mean to say there is no straw in the village?"

"Ah! but this is quite a peculiar straw. If you strew it about even in the hottest summer the air at once becomes cold, and snow falls, and the people freeze."

Then the Simpleton asked him also to join them.

At last the ship, with its strange crew, arrived at the King's Court. The King was having his dinner, but he at once despatched one of his courtiers to find out what the huge, strange new bird could be that had come flying through the air. The courtier peeped into the ship, and, seeing what it was, instantly went back to the King and told him that it was a flying ship, and that it was manned by a few peasants.

Then the King remembered his royal oath; but he made up his mind that he would never consent to let the Princess marry a poor peasant. So he thought and thought, and then said to himself:

"I will give him some impossible tasks to perform; that will be the best way of getting rid of him." And he there and then decided to despatch one of his courtiers to the Simpleton, with the command that he was to fetch the King the healing water from the world's end before he had finished his dinner.

But while the King was still instructing the courtier exactly what he was to say, the first man of the ship's company, the one with the miraculous power of hearing, had overheard the King's words, and hastily reported them to the poor Simpleton.

"Alas, alas!" he cried; "what am I to do now? It would take me quite a year, possibly my whole life, to find the water."

"Never fear," said his fleet-footed comrade, "I will fetch what the King wants."

Just then the courtier arrived, bearing the King's command.

"Tell his Majesty," said the Simpleton, "that his orders shall be obeyed"; and forthwith the swift runner unbound the foot that was strung up behind his ear and started off, and in less than no time had reached the world's end and drawn the healing water from the well.

"Dear me," he thought to himself, "that's rather tiring! I'll just rest for a few minutes; it will be some little time yet before the King has gotten to dessert." So he threw himself down on the grass, and, as the sun was very dazzling, he closed his eyes, and in a few seconds had fallen sound asleep.

In the meantime all the ship's crew were anxiously awaiting him; the King's dinner would soon be finished, and their comrade had not yet returned. So the man with the marvelous quick hearing lay down and, putting his ear to the ground, listened.

"That's a nice sort of fellow!" he suddenly exclaimed. "He's lying on the ground, snoring hard!"

At this the marksman seized his gun, took aim, and fired in the direction of the world's end, in order to awaken the sluggard. And a moment later the swift runner reappeared, and, stepping on board the ship, handed the healing water to the Simpleton. So while the King was still sitting at table finishing his dinner news was brought to him that his orders had been obeyed to the letter.

The Flying Ship

What was to be done now? The King determined to think of a still more impossible task. So he told another courtier to go to the Simpleton with the command that he and his comrades were instantly to eat up twelve oxen and twelve tons of bread. Once more the sharp-eared comrade overheard the King's words while he was still talking to the courtier, and reported them to the Simpleton.

"Alas, alas," he sighed; "what in the world shall I do? Why, it would take us a year, possibly our whole lives, to eat up twelve oxen and twelve tons of bread."

"Never fear," said the glutton. "It will scarcely be enough for me, I'm so hungry."

So when the courtier arrived with the royal message he was told to take back word to the King that his orders should be obeyed. Then twelve roasted oxen and twelve tons of bread were brought alongside of the ship, and at one sitting the glutton had devoured it all.

"I call that a small meal," he said. "I wish they'd brought me some more."

Next, the King ordered that forty casks of wine, containing forty gallons each, were to be drunk up on the spot by the Simpleton and his party. When these words were overheard by the sharp-eared comrade and repeated to the Simpleton, he was in despair.

"Alas, alas!" he exclaimed; "what is to be done? It would take us a year, possibly our whole lives, to drink so much."

"Never fear," said his thirsty comrade. "I'll drink it all up at a gulp, see if I don't." And sure enough, when the forty casks of wine containing forty gallons each were brought alongside of the ship, they disappeared down the thirsty comrade's throat in no time; and when they were empty he remarked:

"Why, I'm still thirsty. I should have been glad of two more casks."

Then the King took counsel with himself and sent an order to the

Simpleton that he was to have a bath, in a bathroom at the royal palace, and after that the betrothal should take place. Now the bathroom was built of iron, and the King gave orders that it was to be heated to such a pitch that it would suffocate the Simpleton. And so when the poor silly youth entered the room, he discovered that the iron walls were red hot. But, fortunately, his comrade with the straw on his back had entered behind him, and when the door was shut upon them he scattered the straw about, and suddenly the red-hot walls cooled down, and it became so very cold that the Simpleton could scarcely bear to take a bath, and all the water in the room froze. So the Simpleton climbed up upon the stove, and, wrapping himself up in the bath blankets, lay there the whole night. And in the morning when they opened the door there he lay sound and safe, singing cheerfully to himself.

Now when this strange tale was told to the King he became quite sad, not knowing what he should do to get rid of so undesirable a son-in-law, when suddenly a brilliant idea occurred to him.

"Tell the rascal to raise me an army, now at this instant!" he exclaimed to one of his courtiers. "Inform him at once of this, my royal will." And to himself he added, "I think I shall do for him this time."

As on former occasions, the quick-eared comrade had overheard the King's command and repeated it to the Simpleton.

"Alas, alas!" he groaned; "now I am quite done for."

"Not at all," replied one of his comrades (the one who had dragged the bundle of wood through the forest). "Have you quite forgotten me?"

In the meantime the courtier, who had run all the way from the palace, reached the ship panting and breathless, and delivered the King's message.

"Good!" remarked the Simpleton. "I will raise an army for the King," and he drew himself up. "But if, after that, the King refuses to accept me as his son-in-law, I will wage war against him, and carry the Princess off by force."

During the night the Simpleton and his comrade went together into a big field, not forgetting to take the bundle of wood with them, which the man spread out in all directions—and in a moment a mighty army stood upon the spot, regiment on regiment of foot and horse soldiers; the bugles sounded and the drums beat, the chargers neighed, and their riders put their lances in rest, and the soldiers presented arms.

In the morning when the King awoke he was startled by these warlike sounds, the bugles and the drums, and the clatter of the horses, and the shouts of the soldiers. And, stepping to the window, he saw the lances gleam in the sunlight and the armor and weapons glitter. And the proud monarch said to himself, "I am powerless in comparison with this man." So he sent him royal robes and costly jewels, and commanded him to come to the palace to be married to the Princess. And his son-in-law put on the royal robes, and he looked so grand and stately that it was impossible to recognize the poor Simpleton, so changed was he; and the Princess fell in love with him as soon as ever she saw him.

Never before had so grand a wedding been seen, and there was so much food and wine that even the glutton and the thirsty comrade had enough to eat and drink.

Hok Lee and the Dwarfs

THERE ONCE LIVED in a small town in China a man named Hok Lee. He was a steady industrious man, who not only worked hard at his trade, but did all his own housework as well, for he had no wife to do it with him. "What an excellent industrious man is this Hok Lee!" said his neighbors; "how hard he works: he never leaves his house to amuse himself or to take a holiday as others do!"

But Hok Lee was by no means the virtuous person his neighbors thought him. True, he worked hard enough by day, but at night, when all respectable folk were fast asleep, he used to steal out and join a dangerous band of robbers, who broke into rich people's houses and carried off all they could lay hands on.

This state of things went on for some time, and, though a thief was caught now and then and punished, no suspicion ever fell on Hok Lee, he was such a *very* respectable, hard-working man.

Hok Lee had already amassed a good store of money as his share of the proceeds of these robberies when it happened one morning on going to market that a neighbor said to him:

"Why, Hok Lee, what is the matter with your face? One side of it is all swelled up."

True enough, Hok Lee's right cheek was twice the size of his left, and it soon began to feel very uncomfortable.

"I will bind up my face," said Hok Lee; "doubtless the warmth will cure the swelling." But no such thing. Next day it was worse, and day by day it grew bigger and bigger till it was nearly as large as his head and became very painful.

Hok Lee was at his wits' ends what to do. Not only was his cheek unsightly and painful, but his neighbors began to jeer and make fun of him, which hurt his feelings very much indeed.

One day, as luck would have it, a traveling doctor came to the town. He sold not only all kinds of medicine, but also dealt in many strange charms against witches and evil spirits.

Hok Lee determined to consult him, and asked him into his house.

After the doctor had examined him carefully, he spoke thus: "This, O Hok Lee, is no ordinary swelled face. I strongly suspect you have been doing some wrong deed which has called down the anger of the spirits on you. None of my drugs will avail to cure you, but, if you are willing to pay me handsomely, I can tell you how you may be cured."

Then Hok Lee and the doctor began to bargain together, and it was a long time before they could come to terms. However, the doctor got the better of it in the end, for he was determined not to part with his secret under a certain price, and Hok Lee had no mind to carry his huge cheek about with him to the end of his days. So he was obliged to part with the greater portion of his ill-gotten gains.

When the doctor had pocketed the money, he told Hok Lee to go on the first night of the full moon to a certain wood and there to watch by a particular tree. After a time he would see the dwarfs and little sprites who live underground come out to dance. When they saw him they would be sure to make him dance too. "And mind you dance your very best," added the doctor. "If you dance well and please them they will grant you a petition and you can then beg to be cured; but if you dance badly they will most likely do you some mischief out of spite." With that he took leave and departed.

Happily the first night of the full moon was near, and at the proper time Hok Lee set out for the wood. With a little trouble he found the tree the doctor had described, and, feeling nervous, he climbed up into it.

He had hardly settled himself on a branch when he saw the little dwarfs assembling in the moonlight. They came from all sides, till at length there appeared to be hundreds of them. They seemed in high glee, and danced and skipped and capered about, whilst Hok Lee grew so eager watching them that he crept farther and farther along his branch till at length it gave a loud crack. All the dwarfs stood still, and Hok Lee felt as if his heart stood still also.

Then one of the dwarfs called out, "Someone is up in that tree. Come down at once, whoever you are, or we must come and fetch you!"

In great terror, Hok Lee proceeded to come down; but he was so nervous that he tripped near the ground and came rolling down in the most absurd manner. When he had picked himself up, he came forward with a low bow, and the dwarf who had first spoken and who appeared to be the leader, said, "Now, then, who art thou, and what brings thee here?"

So Hok Lee told him the sad story of his swelled cheek, and how he had been advised to come to the forest and beg the dwarfs to cure him.

"It is well," replied the dwarf. "We will

see about that. First, however, thou must dance before us. Should thy dancing please us, perhaps we may be able to do something; but shouldst thou dance badly, we shall assuredly punish thee, so now take warning and dance away."

With that, he and all the other dwarfs sat down in a large ring, leaving Hok Lee to dance alone in the middle. He felt half frightened to death, and besides was a good deal shaken by his fall from the tree and did not feel at all inclined to dance. But the dwarfs were not to be trifled with.

"Begin!" cried their leader, and "Begin!" shouted the rest in chorus.

So in despair Hok Lee began. First he hopped on one foot and then on the other, but he was so stiff and so nervous that he made but a poor attempt, and after a time sank down on the ground and vowed he could dance no more.

The dwarfs were very angry. They crowded around Hok Lee and abused him. "Thou to come here to be cured, indeed!" they cried, "thou hast brought one big cheek with thee, but thou shalt take away two." And with that they ran off and disappeared, leaving Hok Lee to find his way home as best he might.

He hobbled away, weary and depressed, and not a little anxious on account of the dwarfs' threat.

Nor were his fears unfounded, for when he rose next morning his left cheek was swelled up as big as his right, and he could hardly see out of his eyes. Hok Lee felt in despair, and his neighbors jeered at him more than ever. The doctor, too, had disappeared, so there was nothing for it but to try the dwarfs once more.

He waited a month till the first night of the full moon came around again, and then he trudged back to the forest, and sat down under the tree from which he had fallen. He had not long to wait. Ere long the dwarfs came trooping out till all were assembled.

"I don't feel quite easy," said one; "I feel as if some horrid human being were near us."

When Hok Lee heard this he came forward and bent down to the ground before the dwarfs, who came crowding around, and laughed heartily at his comical appearance with his two big cheeks.

"What dost thou want?" they asked; and Hok Lee proceeded to tell them of his fresh misfortunes, and begged so hard to be allowed one more trial at dancing that the dwarfs consented, for there is nothing they love so much as being amused.

Now, Hok Lee knew how much depended on his dancing well, so he plucked up a good spirit and began, first quite slowly, and faster by degrees, and he danced so well and gracefully, and made such new and wonderful steps, that the dwarfs were quite delighted with him.

They clapped their tiny hands, and shouted, "Well done, Hok Lee, well done; go on, dance more, for we are pleased."

And Hok Lee danced on and on, till he really could dance no more, and was obliged to stop.

Then the leader of the dwarfs said, "We are well pleased, Hok Lee, and as a recompense for thy dancing thy face shall be cured. Farewell."

With these words he and the other dwarfs vanished, and Hok Lee, putting his hands to his face, found to his great joy that his cheeks were reduced to their natural size. The way home seemed short and easy to him, and he went to bed happy, and resolved never to go out robbing again.

Next day the whole town was full of the news of Hok's sudden cure. His neighbors questioned him, but could get nothing from him, except the fact that he had discovered a wonderful cure for all kinds of diseases.

After a time a rich neighbor, who had been ill for some years, came,

and offered to give Hok Lee a large sum of money if he would tell him how he might get cured. Hok Lee consented on condition that he swore to keep the secret. He did so, and Hok Lee told him of the dwarfs and their dances.

The neighbor went off, carefully obeyed Hok Lee's directions, and was duly cured by the dwarfs. Then another and another came to Hok Lee to beg his secret, and from each he extracted a vow of secrecy and a large sum of money. This went on for some years, so that at length Hok Lee became a very wealthy man, and ended his days in peace and prosperity.

The Hero Makóma

ONCE UPON A TIME, at the town of Senna on the banks of the Zambesi, was born a child. He was not like other children, for he was very tall and strong; over his shoulder he carried a big sack, and in his hand an iron hammer. He could also speak like a grown man, but usually he was very silent.

One day his mother said to him: "My child, by what name shall we know you?"

And he answered: "Call all the head men of Senna here to the river's bank." And his mother called the head men of the town, and when they had come he led them down to a deep black pool in the river where all the fierce crocodiles lived.

"O great men!" he said, while they all listened, "which of you will leap into the pool and overcome the crocodiles?" But no one would come forward. So he turned and sprang into the water and disappeared.

The people held their breath, for they thought: "Surely the boy is bewitched and throws away his life, for the crocodiles will eat him!" Then suddenly the ground trembled, and the pool, heaving and swirling, became red with blood, and presently the boy rising to the surface swam on shore.

But he was no longer just a boy! He was stronger than any man and very tall and handsome, so that the people shouted with gladness when they saw him.

"Now, O my people!" he cried waving his hand, "you know my name—I am Makóma, 'the Greater'; for have I not slain the crocodiles in the pool where none would venture?"

Then he said to his mother: "Rest gently, my mother, for I go to make a home for myself and become a hero." Then, entering his hut he took Nu-éndo, his iron hammer, and throwing the sack over his shoulder, he went away.

Makóma crossed the Zambesi, and for many moons he wandered toward the north and west until he came to a very hilly country where, one day, he met a huge giant making mountains.

"Greeting," shouted Makóma, "who are you?"

"I am Chi-éswa-mapíri, who makes the mountains," answered the giant; "and who are you?"

"I am Makóma, which signifies 'greater,'" answered he.

"Greater than who?" asked the giant.

"Greater than you!" answered Makóma.

The giant gave a roar and rushed upon him. Makóma said nothing, but swinging his great hammer, Nu-éndo, he struck the giant upon the head.

He struck him so hard a blow that the giant shrank into quite a little man, who fell upon his knees saying: "You are indeed greater than I, O Makóma; take me with you to be your slave!" So Makóma picked him up and dropped him into the sack that he carried upon his back.

He was greater than ever now, for all the giant's strength had gone into him; and he resumed his journey, carrying his burden with as little difficulty as an eagle might carry a hare.

Before long he came to a country broken up with huge stones and immense clods of earth. Looking over one of the heaps he saw a giant wrapped in dust dragging out the very earth and hurling it in handfuls on either side of him.

"Who are you," cried Makóma, "that pulls up the earth in this way?"

"I am Chi-dúbula-táka," said he, "and I am making the riverbeds."

"Do you know who I am?" said Makóma. "I am he that is called 'greater'!"

"Greater than who?" thundered the giant.

"Greater than you!" answered Makóma.

With a shout, Chi-dúbula-táka seized a great clod of earth and launched it at Makóma. But the hero had his sack held over his left arm and the stones and earth fell harmlessly upon it, and, tightly gripping his iron hammer, he rushed in and struck the giant to the ground. Chi-dúbula-táka groveled before him, all the while growing smaller and smaller; and when he had become a convenient size Makóma picked him up and put him into the sack beside Chi-éswa-mapíri.

He went on his way even greater than before, as all the river-maker's power had become his; and at last he came to a forest of bao-babs and thorn trees. He was astonished at their size, for every one was full grown and larger than any trees he had ever seen, and close by he saw Chi-gwísa-míti, the giant who was planting the forest.

Chi-gwísa-míti was taller than either of his brothers, but Makóma was not afraid, and called out to him: "Who are you, O Big One?"

"I," said the giant, "am Chi-gwísa-míti, and I am planting these bao-babs and thorns as food for my children the elephants."

"Leave off!" shouted the hero, "for I am Makóma, and would like to exchange a blow with thee!"

The giant, plucking up a monster bao-bab by the roots, struck heavily at Makóma; but the hero sprang aside, and as the weapon sank deep into the soft earth, whirled Nu-éndo the hammer around his head and felled the giant with one blow.

So terrible was the stroke that Chi-gwísa-míti shriveled up as the other giants had done; and when he had got back his breath he begged

Makóma to take him as his servant. "For," said he, "it is honorable to serve a man so great as thou."

Makóma, after placing him in his sack, proceeded upon his journey, and traveling for many days he at last reached a country so barren and rocky that not a single living thing grew upon it—everywhere reigned grim desolation. And in the midst of this dead region he found a man eating fire.

"What are you doing?" demanded Makóma.

"I am eating fire," answered the man, laughing; "and my name is Chi-ídea-móto, for I am the flame-spirit, and can waste and destroy what I like."

"You are wrong," said Makóma; "for I am Makóma, who is 'greater' than you—and you cannot destroy me!"

The fire-eater laughed again, and blew a flame at Makóma. But the hero sprang behind a rock—just in time, for the ground upon which he had been standing was turned to molten glass, like an overbaked pot, by the heat of the flame-spirit's breath.

Then the hero flung his iron hammer at Chi-ídea-móto, and, striking him, it knocked him helpless; so Makóma placed him in the sack, Woro-nówu, with the other great men that he had overcome.

And now, truly, Makóma was a very great hero; for he had the strength to make hills, the industry to lead rivers over dry wastes, foresight and wisdom in planting trees, and the power of producing fire when he wished.

Wandering on he arrived one day at a great plain, well watered and full of game; and in the very middle of it, close to a large river, was a grassy spot, very pleasant to make a home upon.

Makóma was so delighted with the little meadow that he sat down under a large tree, and removing the sack from his shoulder, took out all the giants and set them before him. "My friends," said he, "I have traveled far and am weary. Is not this such a place as would suit a hero for his home? Let us then go, tomorrow, to bring in timber to make a kraal."

So the next day Makóma and the giants set out to get poles to build the kraal, leaving only Chi-éswa-mapíri to look after the place and cook some venison which they had killed. In the evening, when they returned, they found the giant helpless and tied to a tree by one enormous hair!

"How is it," said Makóma, astonished, "that we find you thus bound and helpless?"

"O Chief," answered Chi-éswa-mapíri, "at midday a man came out of the river; he was of immense stature, and his gray mustaches were of such length that I could not see where they ended! He demanded of me 'Who is thy master?' And I answered: 'Makóma, the greatest of heroes.' Then the man seized me, and pulling a hair from his mustache, tied me to this tree—even as you see me."

Makóma was very angry, but he said nothing, and drawing his fingernail across the hair (which was as thick and strong as palm rope) cut it, and set free the mountain-maker.

The three following days exactly the same thing happened, only each time with a different one of the party; and on the fourth day Makóma stayed in camp when the others went to cut poles, saying that he would see for himself what sort of man this was that lived in the river and whose mustaches were so long that they extended beyond men's sight.

So when the giants had gone he swept and tidied the camp and put some venison on the fire to roast. At midday, when the sun was right overhead, he heard a rumbling noise from the river, and looking up he saw the head and shoulders of an enormous man emerging from it. And behold! right down the riverbed and up the riverbed, till they faded into the blue distance, stretched the giant's gray mustaches!

"Who are you?" bellowed the giant, as soon as he was out of the water.

"I am he that is called Makóma," answered the hero; "and, before I slay thee, tell me also what is thy name and what thou doest in the river?"

"My name is Chin-débou Máu-giri," said the giant. "My home is in the river, for my mustache is the gray fever-mist that hangs above the water, and with which I bind all those that come unto me so that they die."

"You cannot bind me!" shouted Makóma, rushing upon him and striking with his hammer. But the river giant was so slimy that the blow slid harmlessly off his green chest, and as Makóma stumbled and tried to regain his balance, the giant swung one of his long hairs around him and tripped him up.

For a moment Makóma was helpless, but remembering the power of the flame-spirit which had entered into him, he breathed a fiery breath upon the giant's hair and cut himself free.

As Chin-débou Máu-giri leaned forward to seize him the hero flung his sack Woro-nówu over the giant's slippery head, and gripping his iron hammer, struck him again; this time the blow alighted upon the dry sack and Chin-débou Máu-giri fell dead.

When the four giants returned at sunset with the poles they rejoiced to find that Makóma had overcome the fever-spirit, and they feasted on the roast venison till far into the night; but in the morning, when they awoke, Makóma was already warming his hands at the fire, and his face was gloomy.

"In the darkness of the night, O my friends," he said presently, "the white spirits of my fathers came unto me and spoke, saying: 'Get thee

hence, Makóma, for thou shalt have no rest until thou hast found and fought with Sákatirína, who has five heads, and is very great and strong; so take leave of thy friends, for thou must go alone."

Then the giants were very sad, and bewailed the loss of their hero; but Makóma comforted them, and gave back to each the gifts he had taken from them. Then bidding them "Farewell," he went on his way.

Makóma traveled far toward the west; over rough mountains and water-logged morasses, fording deep rivers, and tramping for days across dry deserts where most men would have died, until at length he arrived at a hut standing near some large peaks, and inside the hut were two beautiful women.

"Greeting!" said the hero. "Is this the country of Sákatirína of five heads, whom I am seeking?"

"We greet you, O Great One!" answered the women. "We are the wives of Sákatirína; your search is at an end, for there stands he whom you seek!" And they pointed to what Makóma had thought were two tall mountain peaks. "Those are his legs," they said; "his body you cannot see, for it is hidden in the clouds."

Makóma was astonished when he beheld how tall was the giant; but, nothing daunted, he went forward until he reached one of Sákatirína's legs, which he struck heavily with Nu-éndo. Nothing happened, so he hit again and then again until, presently, he heard a tired, far-away voice saying: "Who is it that scratches my feet?"

And Makóma shouted as loud as he could, answering: "It is I, Makóma, who is called 'Greater'!" And he listened, but there was no answer.

Then Makóma collected all the dead brushwood and trees that he could find, and making an enormous pile around the giant's legs, set a light to it.

This time the giant spoke; his voice was very terrible, for it was the rumble of thunder in the clouds. "Who is it," he said, "making that fire smoulder around my feet?"

"It is I, Makóma!" shouted the hero. "And I have come from far away to see thee, O Sákatirína, for the spirits of my fathers bade me go seek and fight with thee, lest I should grow fat, and weary of myself."

There was silence for a while, and then the giant spoke softly: "It is good, O Makóma!" he said. "For I too have grown weary. There is no man so great as I, therefore I am all alone. Guard thyself!" And bending suddenly he seized the hero in his hands and dashed him upon the ground. And lo! instead of death, Makóma had found life, for he sprang to his feet mightier in strength and stature than before, and rushing in he gripped the giant by the waist and wrestled with him.

Hour by hour they fought, and mountains rolled beneath their feet like pebbles in a flood; now Makóma would break away, and summoning up his strength, strike the giant with Nu-éndo his iron hammer, and Sákatirína would pluck up the mountains and hurl them upon the hero, but neither one could slay the other. At last, upon the second day, they grappled so strongly that they could not break away; but their strength was failing, and, just as the sun was sinking, they fell together to the ground, insensible.

In the morning when they awoke, Mulímo the Great Spirit was standing by them; and he said: "O Makóma and Sákatirína! Ye are heroes so great that no man may come against you. Therefore ye will leave the world and take up your home with me in the clouds." And as he spoke the heroes became invisible to the people of the Earth, and were no more seen among them.

The Nixy

❦

THERE WAS ONCE UPON A TIME a miller who was very well off, and had as much money and as many goods as he knew what to do with. But sorrow comes in the night, and the miller all of a sudden became so poor that at last he could hardly call the mill in which he sat his own. He wandered about all day full of despair and misery, and when he lay down at night he could get no rest, but lay awake all night sunk in sorrowful thoughts.

One morning he rose up before dawn and went outside, for he thought his heart would be lighter in the open air. As he wandered up and down on the banks of the mill-pond he heard a rustling in the water, and when he looked near he saw a pale woman rising up from the waves.

He realized at once that this could be none other than the nixy of the mill-pond, and in his terror he didn't know if he should fly away or remain where he was. While he hesitated the nixy spoke, called him by his name, and asked him why he was so sad.

When the miller heard how friendly her tone was, he plucked up heart and told her how rich and prosperous he had been all his life up till now, when he didn't know what he was to do for want and misery.

Then the nixy spoke comforting words to him, and promised that she would make him richer and more prosperous than he had ever been

in his life before, if he would give her in return the youngest thing in his house.

The miller thought she must mean one of his puppies or kittens, so promised the nixy at once what she asked, and returned to his mill full of hope. On the threshold he was greeted by a servant with the news that his wife had just given birth to a boy.

The poor miller was much horrified by these tidings, and went in to his wife with a heavy heart to tell her and his relations of the fatal bargain he had just struck with the nixy. "I would gladly give up all the good fortune she promised me," he said, "if I could only save my child." But no one could think of any advice to give him, beyond taking care that the child never went near the mill-pond.

The Nixy

So the boy throve and grew big, and in the meantime all prospered with the miller, and in a few years he was richer than he had ever been before. But all the same he did not enjoy his good fortune, for he could not forget his compact with the nixy, and he knew that sooner or later she would demand his fulfillment of it. But year after year went by, and the boy grew up and became a great hunter, and the lord of the land took him into his service, for he was as smart and bold a hunter as you would wish to see. In a short time he married a pretty young wife, and lived with her in great peace and happiness.

One day when he was out hunting, a hare sprang up at his feet, and ran for some way in front of him in the open field. The hunter pursued it hotly for some time, and at last shot it dead. Then he proceeded to skin it, never noticing that he was close to the mill-pond, which from childhood up he had been taught to avoid. He soon finished the skinning, and went to the water to wash the blood off his hands. He had hardly dipped them in the pond when the nixy rose up in the water, and seizing him in her wet arms she dragged him down with her under the waves.

When the hunter did not come home in the evening his wife grew very anxious, and when his game bag was found close to the mill-pond she guessed at once what had befallen him. She was nearly beside herself with grief, and roamed around and around the pond calling on her husband without ceasing. At last, worn out with sorrow and fatigue, she fell asleep and dreamed that she was wandering along a flowery meadow, when she came to a hut where she found an old witch, who promised to restore her husband to her.

When she awoke next morning she determined to set out and find the witch; so she wandered on for many a day, and at last she reached the flowery meadow and found the hut where the old witch lived. The poor wife told her all that had happened and how she had been told in a dream of the witch's power to help her.

The witch counseled her to go to the pond the first time there was a full moon, and to comb her black hair with a golden comb, and then to place the comb on the bank. The hunter's wife gave the witch a handsome present, thanked her heartily, and returned home.

Time dragged heavily till the time of the full moon, but it passed at last, and as soon as it rose the young wife went to the pond, combed her black hair with a golden comb, and when she had finished, placed the comb on the bank; then she watched the water impatiently. Soon she heard a rushing sound, and a big wave rose suddenly and swept the comb off the bank, and a minute after the head of her husband rose from the pond and gazed sadly at her. But immediately another wave came, and the head sank back into the water without having said a word. The pond lay still and motionless, glittering in the moonshine, and the hunter's wife was not a bit better off than she had been before.

In despair she wandered about for days and nights, and at last, worn out by fatigue, she sank once more into a deep sleep, and dreamed exactly the same dream about the old witch. So next morning, she went again to the flowery meadow and sought the witch in her hut, and told her of her grief. The old woman counseled her to go to the mill-pond the next full moon and play upon a golden flute, and then to lay the flute on the bank.

As soon as the next moon was full the hunter's wife went to the mill-pond, played on a golden flute, and when she had finished placed it on the bank. Then a rushing sound was heard, and a wave swept the flute off the bank, and soon the head of the hunter appeared and rose up higher and higher till he was half out of the water. Then he gazed sadly at his wife and stretched out his arms toward her. But another rushing wave arose and dragged him under once more. The hunter's wife, who had stood on the bank full of joy and hope, sank into despair when she saw her husband snatched away again before her eyes.

But for her comfort she dreamed the same dream a third time, and betook herself once more to the old witch's hut in the flowery meadow. This time the old woman told her to go the next full moon to the mill-pond, and to spin there with a golden spinning wheel, and then to leave the spinning wheel on the bank.

The hunter's wife did as she was advised, and the first night the moon was full she sat and spun with a golden spinning wheel, and then left the wheel on the bank. In a few minutes a rushing sound was heard in the waters, and a wave swept the spinning wheel from the bank. Immediately the head of the hunter rose up from the pond, getting higher and higher each moment, till at length he stepped on to the bank and fell on his wife's neck.

But the waters of the pond rose up suddenly, overflowed the bank where the couple stood, and dragged them under the flood. In her despair the young wife called on the old witch to help her, and in a moment the hunter was turned into a frog and his wife into a toad. But they were not able to remain together, for the water tore them apart, and when the flood was over they both resumed their own shapes again, but the hunter and the hunter's wife found themselves each in a strange country, and neither knew what had become of the other.

The hunter determined to become a shepherd, and his wife too became a shepherdess. So they herded their sheep for many years in solitude and sadness.

Now it happened once that the shepherd came to the country where the shepherdess lived. The neighborhood pleased him, and he saw that the pasture was rich and suitable for his flocks. So he brought

his sheep there, and herded them as before. The shepherd and shepherdess became great friends, but they did not recognize each other in the least.

But one evening when the moon was full they sat together watching their flocks, and the shepherd played upon his flute. Then the shepherdess thought of that evening when she had sat at the full moon by the mill-pond and had played on the golden flute; the recollection was too much for her, and she burst into tears. The shepherd asked her why she was crying, and left her no peace till she told him all her story. Then the scales fell from the shepherd's eyes, and he recognized his wife, and she him. So they returned joyfully to their own home, and lived in peace and happiness ever after.

The Water of Life

THREE BROTHERS AND ONE SISTER lived together in a small cottage, and they loved one another dearly. One day the eldest brother, who had never done anything but amuse himself from sunrise to sunset, said to the rest, "Let us all work hard, and perhaps we shall grow rich, and be able to build ourselves a palace."

And his brothers and sister answered joyfully, "Yes, we will all work!"

So they fell to working with all their might, till at last they became rich, and were able to build themselves a beautiful palace; and everyone came from miles around to see its wonders, and to say how splendid it was. No one thought of finding any faults, till at length an old woman, who had been walking through the rooms with a crowd of people, suddenly exclaimed, "Yes, it is a splendid palace, but there is still something it needs!"

"And what may that be?"

"A church."

When they heard this the brothers set to work again to earn some more money, and when they had got enough they set about building a church, which should be as large and beautiful as the palace itself.

And after the church was finished greater numbers of people than ever flocked to see the palace and the church and vast gardens and magnificent halls.

But one day, as the brothers were as usual doing the honors to their guests, an old man turned to them and said, "Yes, it is all most beautiful, but there is still something it needs!"

"And what may that be?"

"A pitcher of the water of life, a branch of the tree the smell of whose flowers gives eternal beauty, and the talking bird."

"And where am I to find all those?"

"Go to the mountain that is far off yonder, and you will find what you seek."

After the old man had bowed politely and taken farewell of them the eldest brother said to the rest, "I will go in search of the water of life, and the talking bird, and the tree of beauty."

"But suppose some evil thing befalls you?" asked his sister. "How shall we know?"

"You are right," he replied; "I had not thought of that!"

Then they followed the old man, and said to him, "My eldest brother wishes to seek for the water of life, and the tree of beauty, and the talking bird, that you tell him are needful to make our palace perfect. But how shall we know if any evil thing befalls him?"

So the old man took them a knife, and gave it to them, saying, "Keep this carefully, and as long as the blade is bright all is well; but if the blade is bloody, then know that evil has befallen him."

The brothers thanked him, and departed, and went straight to the palace, where they found the young man making ready to set out for the mountain where the treasures he longed for lay hid.

And he walked, and he walked, and he walked, till he had gone a great way, and there he met a giant.

"Can you tell me how much farther I have still to go before I reach that mountain yonder?"

"And why do you wish to go there?"

"I am seeking the water of life, the talking bird, and a branch of the tree of beauty."

"Many have passed by seeking those treasures, but none have ever come back; and you will never come back either, unless you mark my words. Follow this path, and when you reach the mountain you will find it covered with stones. Do not stop to look at them, but keep on your way. As you go you will hear scoffs and laughs behind you; it will be the stones that mock. Do not heed them; above all, do not turn around. If you do you will become as one of them. Walk straight on till you get to the top, and then take all you wish for."

The young man thanked him for his counsel, and walked, and walked, and walked, till he reached the mountain. And as he climbed he heard behind him scoffs and jeers, but he kept his ears steadily closed to them. At last the noise grew so loud that he lost patience, and he stooped to pick up a stone to hurl into the midst of the clamor, when suddenly his arm seemed to stiffen, and the next moment he was a stone himself!

That day his sister, who thought her brother's steps were long in returning, took out the knife and found the blade was red as blood. Then she cried out to her brothers that something terrible had come to pass.

"I will go and find him," said the second. And he went.

And he walked, and he walked, and he walked, till he met the giant, and asked him if he had seen a young man traveling toward the mountain.

And the giant answered, "Yes, I have seen him pass, but I have not seen him come back. The spell must have worked upon him."

"Then what can I do to disenchant him, and find the water of life, the talking bird, and a branch of the tree of beauty?"

"Follow this path, and when you reach the mountain you will find it

covered with stones. Do not stop to look at them, but climb steadily on. Above all, heed not the laughs and scoffs that will arise on all sides, and never turn around. And when you reach the top you can then take all you desire."

The young man thanked him for his counsel, and set out for the mountain. But no sooner did he reach it than loud jests and gibes broke out on every side, and almost deafened him. For some time he let them rail, and pushed boldly on, till he had passed the place which his brother had gained; then suddenly he thought that among the scoffing sounds he heard his brother's voice. He stopped and looked back; and another stone was added to the number.

Meanwhile the sister left at home was counting the days when her two brothers should return to her. The time seemed long, and it would be hard to say how often she took out the knife and looked at its polished blade to make sure that this one at least was still safe. The blade was always bright and clear; each time she looked she had the happiness of knowing that all was well, till one evening, tired and anxious, as she frequently was at the end of the day, she took it from its drawer, and behold! the blade was red with blood. Her cry of horror brought her youngest brother to her, and, unable to speak, she held out the knife!

"I will go," he said.

So he walked, and he walked, and he walked, until he met the giant, and he asked, "Have two young men, making for yonder mountain, passed this way?"

And the giant answered, "Yes, they have passed by, but they never came back, and by this I know that the spell has fallen upon them."

"Then what must I do to free them, and to get the water of life, and the talking bird, and a branch of the tree of beauty?"

"Go to the mountain, which you will find so thickly covered with stones that you will hardly be able to place your feet, and walk straight forward, turning neither to the right hand nor to the left, and paying no heed to the laughs and scoffs which will follow you, till you reach the top, and then you may take all that you desire."

The young man thanked the giant for his counsel, and set forth to the mountain. And when he began to climb there burst forth all around him a storm of scoffs and jeers; but he thought of the giant's words, and looked neither to the right hand nor to the left, till the mountain top lay straight before him. A moment now and he would have gained it, when, through the groans and yells, he heard his brothers' voices. He turned, and there was one stone the more.

And all this while his sister was pacing up and down the palace, hardly letting the knife out of her hand, and dreading what she knew she would see, and what she *did* see. The blade grew red before her eyes, and she said, "Now it is my turn."

So she walked, and she walked, and she walked till she came to the giant, and prayed him to tell her if he had seen three young men pass that way seeking the distant mountain.

"I have seen them pass, but they have never returned, and by this I know that the spell has fallen upon them."

"And what must I do to set them free, and to find the water of life, and the talking bird, and a branch of the tree of beauty?"

"You must go to that mountain, which is so full of stones that your feet will hardly find a place to tread, and as you climb you will hear a noise as if all the stones in the world were mocking you; but pay no heed to anything you may hear, and, once you gain the top, you have gained everything."

The girl thanked him for his counsel, and set out for the mountain; and scarcely had she gone a few steps upward when cries and screams broke forth around her, and she felt as if each stone she trod on was a living thing. But she remembered the words of the giant, and knew not what had befallen her brothers, and kept her face steadily toward the mountain top, which grew nearer and nearer every moment. But as she mounted the clamor increased sevenfold: high above them all rang the voices of her three brothers. But the girl took no heed, and at last her feet stood upon the top.

Then she looked around, and saw, lying in a hollow, the pool of the water of life. And she took the brazen pitcher that she had brought with her, and filled it to the brim. By the side of the pool stood the tree of beauty, with the talking bird on one of its boughs; and she caught the bird, and placed it in a cage, and broke off one of the branches.

After that she turned, and went joyfully down the hill again, carrying her treasures, but her long climb had tired her out, and the brazen pitcher was very heavy, and as she walked a few drops of the

water spilled on the stones, and as it touched them they changed into young men and maidens, crowding about her to give thanks for their deliverance.

So she learned by this how the evil spell might be broken, and she carefully sprinkled every stone till there was not one left—only a great company of youths and girls who followed her down the mountain.

When they arrived at the palace she did not lose a moment in planting the branch of the tree of beauty and watering it with the water of life. And the branch shot up into a tree, and was heavy with flowers, and the talking bird nestled in its branches.

Now the fame of these wonders was noised abroad, and the people flocked in great numbers to see the three marvels, and the maiden who had won them; and among the sightseers came the king's son, who would not go till everything was shown him, and till he had heard how it had all happened. And the prince admired the strangeness and beauty of the treasures in the palace, but more than all he admired the beauty and courage of the maiden who had brought them there. So he went home and told his parents, and gained their consent to wed her for his wife.

Then the marriage was celebrated in the church adjoining the palace. Then the bridegroom took her to his own home, where they lived happy for ever after.

The Nightingale

IN CHINA, as I daresay you know, the Emperor is a Chinaman, and all his courtiers are also Chinamen. The story I am going to tell you happened many years ago, but it is worthwhile for you to listen to it, before it is forgotten.

The Emperor's palace was the most splendid in the world, all made of priceless porcelain, but so brittle and delicate that you had to take great care how you touched it. In the garden were the most beautiful flowers, and on the loveliest of them were tied silver bells which tinkled, so that if you passed you could not help looking at the flowers. Everything in the Emperor's garden was admirably arranged with a view to effect; and the garden was so large that even the gardener himself did not know where it ended. If you ever got beyond it, you came to a stately forest with great trees and deep lakes in it. The forest sloped down to the sea, which was a clear blue. Large ships could sail under the boughs of the trees, and in these trees there lived a Nightingale. She sang so beautifully that even the poor fisherman who had so much to do stood and listened when he came at night to cast his nets. "How beautiful it is!" he said; but he had to attend to his work, and forgot about the bird. But when she sang the next night and the fisherman came there again, he said the same thing, "How beautiful it is!"

From all the countries around came travelers to the Emperor's town, who were astonished at the palace and the garden. But when they heard the Nightingale they all said, "This is the finest thing after all!"

The travelers told all about it when they went home, and learned scholars wrote many books upon the town, the palace, and the garden. But they did not forget the Nightingale; she was praised the most, and all the poets composed splendid verses on the Nightingale in the forest by the deep sea.

The books were circulated throughout the world, and some of them reached the Emperor. He sat in his golden chair, and read and read. He nodded his head every moment, for he liked reading the brilliant accounts of the town, the palace, and the garden. "But the Nightingale is better than all," he saw written.

"What is that?" said the Emperor. "I don't know anything about the Nightingale! Is there such a bird in my empire, and so near as in my garden? I have never heard it! Fancy reading for the first time about it in a book!"

And he called his First Lord to him. He was so proud that if anyone of lower rank than his own ventured to speak to him or ask him anything, he would say nothing but "P!" and that does not mean anything.

"Here is a most remarkable bird which is called a Nightingale!" said the Emperor. "They say it is the most glorious thing in my kingdom. Why has no one ever said anything to me about it?"

"I have never before heard it mentioned!" said the First Lord. "I will look for it and find it!"

But where was it to be found? The First Lord ran up and down stairs, through the halls and corridors; but none of those he met had ever heard of the Nightingale. And the First Lord ran again to the Emperor, and told him that it must be an invention on the part of those who had written the books.

"Your Imperial Majesty cannot really believe all that is written!

The Nightingale

There are some inventions called the Black Art!"

"But the book in which I read this," said the Emperor, "is sent me by His Great Majesty the Emperor of Japan; so it cannot be untrue, and I will hear the Nightingale! She must be here this evening! She has my gracious permission to appear, and if she does not, the whole Court shall be trampled under foot after supper!"

"Tsing pe!" said the First Lord; and he ran up and down stairs, through the halls and corridors, and half the Court ran with him, for they did not want to be trampled under foot. Everyone was asking after the wonderful Nightingale which all the world knew of, except those at Court.

At last they met a poor little girl in the kitchen, who said, "Oh! I know the Nightingale well. How she sings! I have permission to carry the scraps over from the Court meals to my poor sick mother, and when I am going home at night, tired and weary, and rest for a little in the wood, then I hear the Nightingale singing! It brings tears to my eyes, and I feel as if my mother were kissing me!"

"Little kitchenmaid!" said the First Lord, "I will give you a place in the kitchen, and you shall have leave to see the Emperor at dinner, if you can lead us to the Nightingale, for she is invited to come to Court this evening."

And so they all went into the wood where the Nightingale was wont to sing, and half the Court went too.

When they were on the way there they heard a cow mooing.

"Oh!" said the Courtiers, "now we have found her! What a wonderful power for such a small beast to have! I am sure we have heard her before!"

"No; that is a cow mooing!" said the little kitchenmaid. "We are still a long way off!"

Then the frogs began to croak in the marsh. "Splendid!" said the

Chinese chaplain. "Now we hear her; it sounds like a little church-bell!"

"No, no; those are frogs!" said the little kitchenmaid. "But I think we shall soon hear her now!"

Then the Nightingale began to sing.

"There she is!" cried the little girl. "Listen! She is sitting there!" And she pointed to a little dark-gray bird up in the branches.

"Is it possible!" said the First Lord. "I should never have thought it! How ordinary she looks! She must surely have lost her feathers because she sees so many distinguished men around her!"

"Little Nightingale," called out the little kitchenmaid, "our Gracious Emperor wants you to sing before him!"

"With the greatest of pleasure!" said the Nightingale; and she sang so gloriously that it was a pleasure to listen.

"It sounds like glass bells!" said the First Lord. "And look how her little throat works! It is wonderful that we have never heard her before! She will be a great success at Court."

"Shall I sing once more for the Emperor?" asked the Nightingale, thinking that the Emperor was there.

"My esteemed little Nightingale," said the First Lord, "I have the great pleasure to invite you to Court this evening, where His Gracious Imperial Highness will be enchanted with your charming song!"

"It sounds best in the green wood," said the Nightingale; but still, she came gladly when she heard that the Emperor wished it. At the palace everything was splendidly prepared. The porcelain walls and floors glittered in the light of many thousand gold lamps; the most gorgeous flowers which tinkled out well were placed in the corridors. There was such a hurrying and draft that all the bells jingled so much that one could not hear oneself speak. In the center of the great hall where the Emperor sat was a golden perch, on which the Nightingale sat. The whole Court was there, and the little kitchenmaid was allowed to stand behind the door, now that she was a Court cook. Everyone was dressed in his best, and everyone was looking toward the little gray bird to whom the Emperor nodded.

The Nightingale sang so gloriously that the tears came into the Emperor's eyes and ran down his cheeks. Then the Nightingale sang even more beautifully; it went straight to all hearts. The Emperor was so delighted that he said she should wear his gold slipper around her neck. But the Nightingale thanked him, and said she had had enough reward already. "I have seen tears in the Emperor's eyes—that is a great reward. An Emperor's tears have such power!" Then she sang again with her gloriously sweet voice.

"That is the most charming coquetry I have ever seen!" said all the ladies around. And they all took to holding water in their mouths that they might gurgle whenever anyone spoke to them. Then they thought themselves nightingales. Yes, the lackeys and chambermaids announced that they were pleased; which means a great deal, for they are the most difficult people of all to satisfy. In short, the Nightingale was a real success.

She had to stay at Court now; she had her own cage, and permission to walk out twice in the day and once at night.

She was given twelve servants, who each held a silken string which was fastened around her leg. There was little pleasure in flying about like this.

The whole town was talking about the wonderful bird, and when two people met each other one would say "Nightin," and the other "Gale," and then they would both sigh and understand one another. Yes, and eleven grocer's children were called after her, but not one of them could sing a note.

The Nightingale

One day the Emperor received a large parcel on which was written "The Nightingale."

"Here is another new book about our famous bird!" said the Emperor.

But it was not a book, but a little mechanical toy, which lay in a box—an artificial nightingale which was like the real one, only that it was set all over with diamonds, rubies, and sapphires. When it was wound up, it could sing the piece the real bird sang, and moved its tail up and down, and glittered with silver and gold. Around its neck was a little collar on which was written, "The Nightingale of the Emperor of Japan is nothing compared to that of the Emperor of China."

"This is magnificent!" they all said, and the man who had brought the clockwork bird received on the spot the title of "Bringer of the Imperial First Nightingale."

"Now they must sing together; what a duet we shall have!"

And so they sang together, but their voices did not blend, for the real Nightingale sang in her way and the clockwork bird sang waltzes.

"It is not its fault!" said the bandmaster; "it keeps very good time and is quite after my style!"

Then the artificial bird had to sing alone. It gave just as much pleasure as the real one, and then it was so much prettier to look at; it sparkled like bracelets and necklaces. Three-and-thirty times it sang the same piece without being tired. People would like to have heard it again, but the Emperor thought that the living Nightingale should sing now—but where was she? No one had noticed that she had flown out of the open window away to her green wood.

"What *shall* we do!" said the Emperor.

And all the Court scolded, and said that the Nightingale was very ungrateful. "But we have still the best bird!" they said and the artificial bird had to sing again, and that was the thirty-fourth time they had heard the same piece. But they did not yet know it by heart; it was much too difficult. And the bandmaster praised the bird tremendously; yes, he assured them it was better than a real nightingale, not only because of its beautiful plumage and diamonds, but inside as well. "For see, my Lords and Ladies and your Imperial Majesty, with the real Nightingale one can never tell what will come out, but all is known about the artificial bird: You can explain it, you can open it and show people where the waltzes lie, how they go, and how one follows the other!"

"That's just what we think!" said everyone; and the bandmaster received permission to show the bird to the people the next Sunday. They should hear it sing, commanded the Emperor. And they heard it, and they were as pleased as if they had been intoxicated with tea, after the Chinese fashion, and they all said "Oh!" and held up their forefingers and nodded time. But the poor fisherman who had heard the real Nightingale said: "This one sings well enough, the tunes glide out; but there is something wanting—I don't know what!"

The real Nightingale was banished from the kingdom.

The artificial bird was put on silken cushions by the Emperor's bed, all the presents which it received, gold and precious stones, lay around it, and it was given the title of Imperial Night-singer, First from the left. For the Emperor counted that side as the more distinguished, being the side on which the heart is; the Emperor's heart is also on the left.

And the bandmaster wrote a work of twenty-five volumes about the artificial bird. It was so learned, long, and so full of the hardest Chinese words that everyone said they had read it and understood it; for once they had been very stupid about a book, and had been trampled underfoot in consequence. So a whole year passed. The Emperor, the Court, and all the Chinese knew every note of the artificial bird's song by heart. But they liked it all the better for this; they could even sing with it, and they did. The street boys sang, "Tra-la-la-la-la," and the Emperor sang too sometimes. It was indeed delightful.

But one evening, when the artificial bird was singing its best, and the Emperor lay in bed listening to it, something in the bird went crack. Something snapped! Whir-r-r! all the wheels ran down and then the music ceased. The Emperor sprang up, and had his physician summoned, but what could *he* do! Then the clockmaker came, and, after a great deal of talking and examining, he put the bird somewhat in order, but he said that it must be very seldom used as the works were nearly worn out, and it was impossible to put in new ones. Here was a calamity! Only once a year was the artificial bird allowed to sing, and even that was almost too much for it. But then the bandmaster made a little speech full of hard words, saying that it was just as good as before. And so, of course, it *was* just as good as before. So five years passed, and then a great sorrow came to the nation. The Chinese look upon their Emperor as everything, and now he was ill, and not likely to live it was said.

Already a new Emperor had been chosen, and the people stood outside in the street and asked the First Lord how the old Emperor was. "P!" said he, and shook his head.

Cold and pale lay the Emperor in his splendid great bed; the whole Court believed him dead, and one after the other left him to pay their respects to the new Emperor. Everywhere in the halls and corridors cloth was laid down so that no footstep could be heard, and everything was still—very, very still. And nothing came to break the silence.

The Emperor longed for something to come and relieve the monotony of this deathlike stillness. If only someone would speak to him! If only someone would sing to him. Music would carry his thoughts away, and would break the spell lying on him. The moon was streaming in at the open window; but that, too, was silent, quite silent.

"Music! music!" cried the Emperor. "You little bright golden bird, sing! do sing! I gave you gold and jewels; I have hung my gold slipper around your neck with my own hand—sing! do sing!" But the bird was silent. There was no one to wind it up, and so it could not sing. And all was silent, so terribly silent!

All at once there came in at the window the most glorious burst of song. It was the little living Nightingale, who, sitting outside on a bough, had heard the need of her Emperor and had come to sing to him of comfort and hope. And as she sang the blood flowed quicker and quicker in the Emperor's weak limbs, and life began to return.

"Thank you, thank you!" said the Emperor. "You divine little bird! I know you. I chased you from my kingdom, and you have given me life again! How can I reward you?"

"You have done that already!" said the Nightingale. "I brought tears to your eyes the first time I sang. I shall never forget that. They are jewels that rejoice a singer's heart. But now sleep and get strong again; I will sing you a lullaby." And the Emperor fell into a deep, calm sleep as she sang.

The sun was shining through the window when he awoke, strong and well. None of his servants had come back yet, for they thought he was dead. But the Nightingale sat and sang to him.

"You must always stay with me!" said the Emperor. "You shall sing whenever you like, and I will break the artificial bird into a thousand pieces."

"Don't do that!" said the Nightingale. "He did his work as long as he could. Keep him as you have done! I cannot build my nest in the palace and live here; but let me come whenever I like. I will sit in the

evening on the bough outside the window, and I will sing you something that will make you feel happy and grateful. I will sing of joy, and of sorrow; I will sing of the evil and the good which lies hidden from you. The little singing-bird flies all around, to the poor fisherman's hut, to the farmer's cottage, to all those who are far away from you and your Court. I love your heart more than your crown, though that has about it a brightness as of something holy. Now I will sing to you again; but you must promise me one thing—"

"Anything!" said the Emperor, standing up in his Imperial robes, which he had himself put on, and fastening on his sword richly embossed with gold.

"One thing I beg of you! Don't tell anyone that you have a little bird who tells you everything. It will be much better not to!" Then the Nightingale flew away.

The servants came in to look at their dead Emperor.

The Emperor said, "Good morning!"

The Master Cat

or Puss in Boots

THERE WAS A MILLER who left no more estate to the three sons he had than his mill, his ass, and his cat. The partition was soon made. Neither the scrivener nor attorney was sent for. They would soon have eaten up all the poor patrimony. The eldest had the mill, the second the ass, and the youngest nothing but the Cat.

The poor young fellow was quite comfortless at having so poor a lot.

"My brothers," said he, "may get their living handsomely enough by joining their stocks together; but, for my part, when I have eaten up my cat, and made me a muff of his skin, I must die of hunger."

The Cat, who heard all this, but made as if he did not, said to him with a grave and serious air:

"Do not thus afflict yourself, my good master; you have nothing else to do but to give me a bag, and get a pair of boots made for me, that I may scamper through the dirt and the brambles, and you shall see that you have not so bad a portion of me as you imagine."

The Cat's master did not build very much upon what he said; he had, however, often seen him play a great many cunning tricks to catch rats and mice; as when he used to hang by the heels, or hide himself in the meal, and make as if he were dead; so that he did not altogether despair of his affording him some help in his miserable condition. When the Cat had what he asked for, he booted himself very gallantly, and, putting his bag about his neck, he held the strings of it in his two forepaws, and went into a warren where there was a great abundance of rabbits. He put bran and sow-thistle into his bag, and, stretching out at length, as if he had been dead, he waited for some young rabbits, not yet acquainted with the deceits of the world, to come and rummage his bag for what he had put into it.

Scarce was he lain down but he had what he wanted: a rash and foolish young rabbit jumped into his bag and Monsieur Puss, immediately drawing close the strings, took and killed him without pity. Proud of his prey, he went with it to the palace, and asked to speak with his Majesty. He was shown upstairs into the King's apartment, and, making a low reverence, said to him:

"I have brought you, sir, a rabbit of the warren, which my noble Lord, the Master of Carabas" (for that was the title which Puss was pleased to give his master) "has commanded me to present to your Majesty from him."

"Tell thy master," said the King, "that I thank him, and that he does me a great deal of pleasure."

Another time he went and hid himself among some standing corn, holding still his bag open; and, when a brace of partridges ran into it, he drew the strings, and so caught them both. He went and made a present of these to the King, as he had done before of the rabbit which he took in the warren. The King, in like manner, received the partridges with great pleasure, and ordered him some money, to drink.

The Cat continued for two or three months thus to carry his Majesty, from time to time, game of his master's taking. One day in particular, when he knew for certain that he was to take the air along the riverside, with his daughter, the most beautiful princess in the world, he said to his master:

"If you will follow my advice your fortune is made. You have nothing else to do but go and wash yourself in the river, in that part I shall show you, and leave the rest to me."

The Marquis of Carabas did what the Cat advised him to, without knowing why or wherefore. While he was washing the King passed by, and the Cat began to cry out:

"Help! help! My Lord Marquis of Carabas is going to be drowned."

At this noise the King put his head out of the coach window, and, finding it was the Cat who had so often brought him such good game, he commanded his guards to run immediately to the assistance of his Lordship the Marquis of Carabas. While they were drawing the poor Marquis out of the river, the Cat came up to the coach and told the King that, while his master was washing, there came by some rogues, who went off with his clothes, though he had cried out: "Thieves! thieves!" several times, as loud as he could.

This cunning Cat had hidden them under a great stone. The King immediately commanded the officers of his wardrobe to run and fetch one of his best suits for the Lord Marquis of Carabas.

The King caressed him after a very extraordinary manner, and as the fine clothes he had given him extremely set off his good mien (for he was well made and very handsome in his person), the King's daughter took a secret inclination to him, and the Marquis of Carabas had no sooner cast two or three respectful and somewhat tender glances but she fell in love with him to distraction. The King would needs have him come into the coach and take part of the airing. The Cat, quite overjoyed to see his project begin to succeed, marched on before, and, meeting with some countrymen, who were mowing a meadow, he said to them:

"Good people, you who are mowing, if you do not tell the King that the meadow you mow belongs to my Lord Marquis of Carabas, you shall be chopped as small as herbs for the pot."

The King did not fail asking of the mowers to whom the meadow they were mowing belonged.

"To my Lord Marquis of Carabas," answered they altogether, for the Cat's threats had made them terribly afraid.

"You see, sir," said the Marquis, "this is a meadow which never fails to yield a plentiful harvest every year."

The Master Cat, who went still on before, met with some reapers, and said to them:

"Good people, you who are reaping, if you do not tell the King that all this corn belongs to the Marquis of Carabas, you shall be chopped as small as herbs for the pot."

The King, who passed by a moment after, would needs know to whom all that corn, which he then saw, did belong.

"To my Lord Marquis of Carabas," replied the reapers, and the King

was very well pleased with it, as well as the Marquis, whom he con-gratulated thereupon. The Master Cat, who went always before, said the same words to all he met, and the King was astonished at the vast estates of my Lord Marquis of Carabas.

Monsieur Puss came at last to a stately castle, the master of which was an ogre, the richest had ever been known; for all the lands which the King had then gone over belonged to this castle. The Cat, who had taken care to inform himself who this ogre was and what he could do, asked to speak with him, saying he could not pass so near his castle without having the honor of paying his respects to him.

The ogre received him as civilly as an ogre could do, and made him sit down.

"I have been assured," said the Cat, "that you have the gift of being able to change yourself into all sorts of creatures you have a mind to; you can, for example, transform yourself into a lion, or elephant, and the like."

"That is true," answered the ogre very briskly; "and to convince you, you shall see me now become a lion."

Puss was so sadly terrified at the sight of a lion so near him that he immediately got into the gutter, not without abundance of trouble and danger, because of his boots, which were of no use at all to him in walking upon the tiles. A little while after, when Puss saw that the ogre had resumed his natural form, he came down, and owned he had been very much frightened.

"I have been moreover informed," said the Cat, "but I know not how to believe it, that you have also the power to take on you the shape of the smallest animals; for example, to change yourself into a rat or a mouse; but I must own to you I take this to be impossible."

"Impossible!" cried the ogre; "you shall see that presently."

And at the same time he changed himself into a mouse, and began to run about the floor. Puss no sooner perceived this but he fell upon him and ate him up.

Meanwhile the King, who saw, as he passed, this fine castle of the ogre's, had a mind to go into it. Puss, who heard the noise of his Majesty's coach running over the drawbridge, ran out, and said to the King:

"Your Majesty is welcome to this castle of my Lord Marquis of Carabas."

"What! my Lord Marquis," cried the King, "and does this castle also belong to you? There can be nothing finer than this court and all the stately buildings which surround it; let us go into it, if you please."

The Marquis gave his hand to the Princess, and followed the King, who went first. They passed into a spacious hall, where they found a magnificent collation, which the ogre had prepared for his friends, who were that very day to visit him, but dared not to enter, knowing the King was there. His Majesty was perfectly charmed with the good qualities of my Lord Marquis of Carabas, as was his daughter, who had fallen violently in love with him, and, seeing the vast estate he possessed, said to him, after having drunk five or six glasses:

"It will be owing to yourself only, my Lord Marquis, if you are not my son-in-law."

The Marquis, making several low bows, accepted the honor which his Majesty conferred upon him, and forthwith, that very same day, married the Princess.

Puss became a great lord, and never ran after mice any more but only for his diversion.

Father Grumbler

ONCE UPON A TIME there lived a man who had nearly as many children as there were sparrows in the garden. He had to work very hard all day to get them enough to eat, and was often tired and cross, and abused everything and everybody, so that people called him "Father Grumbler."

By-and-by he grew weary of always working, and on Sundays he lay a long while in bed, instead of going to church. Then after a time he found it dull to sit so many hours by himself, thinking of nothing but how to pay the rent that was owing, and as the tavern across the road looked bright and cheerful, he walked in one day and sat down with his friends. "It was just to chase away Care," he said; but when he came out, hours and hours after, Care came out with him.

Father Grumbler entered his house feeling more dismal than when he left it, for he knew that he had wasted both his time and money.

"I will go and see the Holy Man in the cave near the well," he said to himself, "and perhaps he can tell me why all the luck is for other people, and only misfortunes happen to me." And he set out at once for the cave.

It was a long way off, and the road led over mountains and through valleys; but at last he reached the cave where the Holy Man dwelt, and knocked at the door.

"Who is there?" asked a voice from within.

"It is I, Holy Man, Father Grumbler, you know, who has as many children as sparrows in the garden."

"Well, and what is it that you want?"

"I want to know why other people have all the luck, and only misfortunes happen to me!"

The Holy Man did not answer, but went into an inner cave, from which he came out bearing something in his hand. "Do you see this basket?" said he. "It is a magical basket, and if you are hungry you have only got to say: 'Little basket, little basket, do your duty,' and you will eat the best dinner you ever had in your life. But when you have had enough, be sure you don't forget to cry out: 'That will do for today.' Oh!—and one thing more—you need not show it to everybody and declare that I have given it to you. Do you understand?"

Father Grumbler was always accustomed to think of himself as so unlucky that he did not know whether the Holy Man was not playing a trick upon him; but he took the basket without being polite enough to say either "Thank you," or "Good morning," and went away. However, he only waited till he was out of sight of the cave before he stooped down and whispered: "Little basket, little basket, do your duty."

Now the basket had a lid, so that he could not see what was inside, but he heard quite clearly strange noises, as if a sort of scuffling was going on. Then the lid burst open, and a quantity of delicious little white rolls came tumbling out one after the other, followed by a stream of small dishes all ready cooked. What a quantity there were to be sure! The whole road was covered with them, and the banks on each side were beginning to disappear. Father Grumbler felt quite frightened at the torrent, but at last he remembered what the Holy Man had told him, and cried at the top of his voice: "Enough! enough! That will do

for today!" And the lid of the basket closed with a snap.

Father Grumbler sighed with relief and happiness as he looked around him, and sitting down on a heap of stones, he ate till he could eat no more. Trout, salmon, turbot, soles, and a hundred other fishes whose names he did not know lay boiled, fried, and grilled within reach of his hands. As the Holy Man had said, he had never eaten such a dinner; still, when he had done, he shook his head, and grumbled: "Yes, there is plenty to eat, of course, but it only makes me thirsty, and there is not a drop to drink anywhere."

Yet, somehow, he could never tell why, he looked up and saw the tavern in front of him, which he thought was miles, and miles, and miles away.

"Bring the best wine you have got, and two glasses, good mother," he said as he entered, "and if you are fond of fish there is enough here to feed the house. Only there is no need to chatter about it all over the place. You understand? Eh?" And without waiting for an answer he whispered to the basket: "Little basket, little basket, do your duty." The innkeeper and his wife thought that their customer had gone suddenly mad, and watched him closely, ready to spring on him if he became violent; but both instinctively jumped backward, nearly into the fire, as rolls and fishes of every kind came tumbling out of the basket, covering the tables and chairs and the floor, and even overflowing into the street.

"Be quick, be quick, and pick them up," cried the man. And if these are not enough, there are plenty more to be had for the asking."

The innkeeper and his wife did not need telling twice. Down they went on their knees and gathered up everything they could lay hands on. But busy though they seemed, they found time to whisper to each other:

"If we can only get hold of that basket it will make our fortune!"

So they began by inviting Father Grumbler to sit down to the table, and brought out the best wine in the cellar, hoping it might loosen his tongue. But Father Grumbler was wiser than they gave him credit for, and though they tried in all manner of ways to find out who had given him the basket, he put them off, and kept his secret to himself. Unluckily, though he did not *speak*, he did drink, and it was not long before he fell fast asleep. Then the woman fetched from her kitchen a basket, so like the magic one that no one, without looking very closely, could tell the difference, and placed it in Father Grumbler's hand, while she hid the other carefully away.

It was dinner time when the man awoke, and, jumping up hastily, he set out for home, where he found all the children gathered around a basin of thin soup, and pushing their wooden bowls forward, hoping to have the first spoonful. Their father burst into the midst of them, bearing his basket, and crying:

"Don't spoil your appetites, children, with that stuff. Do you see this basket? Well, I have only got to say, 'Little basket, little basket, do your duty,' and you will see what will happen. Now you shall say it instead of me, for a treat."

The children, wondering and delighted, repeated the words, but nothing happened. Again and again they tried, but the basket was only a basket, with a few scales of fish sticking to the bottom, for the innkeeper's wife had taken it to market the day before.

"What is the matter with the thing?" cried the father at last, snatching the basket from them, and turning it all over, grumbling and swearing while he did so, under the eyes of his astonished wife and children, who did not know whether to cry or to laugh.

"It certainly smells of fish," he said, and then he stopped, for a sudden thought had come to him.

"Suppose it is not mine at all; supposing—Ah, the scoundrels!"

Father Grumbler

And without listening to his wife and children, who were frightened at his strange conduct and begged him to stay at home, he ran across to the tavern and burst open the door.

"Can I do anything for you, Father Grumbler?" asked the innkeeper's wife in her softest voice.

"I have taken the wrong basket—by mistake, of course," said he. "Here is yours, will you give me back my own?"

"Why, what are you talking about?" answered she. "You can see for yourself that there is no basket here."

And though Father Grumbler *did* look, it was quite true that none was to be seen.

"Come, take a glass to warm you this cold day," said the woman, who was anxious to keep him in a good temper, and as this was an invitation Father Grumbler never refused, he tossed it off and left the house.

He took the road that led to the Holy Man's cave, and made such haste that it was not long before he reached it.

"Who is there?" said a voice in answer to his knock.

"It is me, it is me, Holy Man. You know quite well. Father Grumbler, who has as many children as sparrows in the garden."

"But, my good man, it was only yesterday that I gave you a handsome present."

"Yes, Holy Man, and here it is. But something has happened, I don't know what, and it won't work any more.

"Well, put it down. I will go and see if I can find anything for you."

In a few minutes the Holy Man returned with a cock under his arm.

"Listen to me," he said, "whenever you want money, you have only to say: 'Show me what you can do, cock,' and you will see some wonderful things. But, remember, it is not necessary to let all the world into the secret."

"Oh no, Holy Man, I am not so foolish as that."

"Nor to tell everybody that I gave it to you," went on the Holy Man. "I have not got these treasures by the dozen."

And without waiting for an answer he shut the door.

As before, the distance seemed to have wonderfully shortened, and in a moment the tavern rose up in front of Father Grumbler. Without stopping to think, he went straight in, and found the innkeeper's wife in the kitchen making a cake.

"Where have you come from, with that fine red cock in your basket?" asked she, for the bird was so big that the lid would not shut down properly.

"Oh, I come from a place where they don't keep these things by the dozen," he replied, sitting down in front of the table.

The woman said no more, but set before him a bottle of his favorite wine, and soon he began to wish to display his prize.

"Show me what you can do, cock," cried he. And the cock stood up and flapped his wings three times, crowing "coquerico" with a voice like a trumpet, and at each crow there fell from his beak golden drops, and diamonds as large as peas.

This time Father Grumbler did not invite the innkeeper's wife to pick up his treasures, but put his own hat under the cock's beak, so as to catch everything he let fall; and he did not see the husband and wife exchanging glances with each other which said, "That would be a splendid cock to put with our basket."

"Have another glass of wine?" suggested the innkeeper, when they had finished admiring the beauty of the cock, for they pretended not to have seen the gold or the diamonds. And Father Grumbler, nothing loth, drank one glass after another, till his head fell forward on the table, and once more he was sound asleep. Then the woman gently coaxed the cock from the basket and carried it off to her own poultry yard, from which she brought one exactly like it, and popped it in its place.

Night was falling when the man awoke, and throwing proudly some grains of gold on the table to pay for the wine he had drunk, he tucked the cock comfortably into his basket and set out for home.

His wife and all the children were waiting for him at the door, and as soon as she caught sight of him she broke out:

"You are a nice man to go wasting your time and your money drinking in that tavern, and leaving us to starve! Aren't you ashamed of yourself?"

"You don't know what you are talking of," he answered. "Money? Why, I have gold and diamonds now, as much as I want. Do you see that cock? Well, you have only to say to him, 'Show what you can do, cock,' and something splendid will happen."

Neither wife nor children were inclined to put much faith in him after their last experience; however, they thought it was worth trying, and did as he told them. The cock flew round the room like a mad thing, and crowed till their heads nearly split with the noise; but no gold or diamonds dropped on the brick floor—not the tiniest grain of either.

Father Grumbler stared in silence for an instant, and then he began

to swear so loudly that even his
family, accustomed as they were
to his language, wondered at
him.

At last he grew a little quieter, but remained as puzzled as
ever.

"Can I have forgotten the
words? But I *know* that was what
he said! And I saw the diamonds
with my own eyes!" Then suddenly he seized the cock, shut it
into the basket, and rushed out
of the house.

His heavy wooden shoes clat-
tered as he ran along the road, and he made such haste that the stars
were only just beginning to come out when he reached the cave of the
Holy Man.

"Who is that knocking?" asked a voice from within

"It is me! It is me! Holy Man! you know! Father—"

"But, my good fellow, you really should give some one else a chance.
This is the third time you have been—and at such an hour, too!"

"Oh, yes, Holy Man, I know it is very late, but you will forgive me!
It is your cock—there is something the matter. It is like the basket.
Look!"

"*That* my cock? *That* my basket? Somebody has played you a trick,
my good man!"

"A trick?" repeated Father Grumbler, who began to understand what
had happened. "Then it must have been those two—"

"I warned you not to show them to anybody," said the Holy Man. "You deserve—but I will give you one more chance." And, turning he unhooked something from the wall.

"When you wish to dust your own jacket or those of your friends," he said, "you have only got to say, 'Flack, flick, switch, be quick,' and you will see what happens. That is all I have to tell you." And, smiling to himself, the Holy Man pushed Father Grumbler out of the cave.

"Ah, I understand now," muttered the good man, as he took the road home; "but I think I have got you two rascals!" and he hurried off to the tavern with his basket under his arm, and the cock and the switch both inside.

"Good evening, friends!" he said, as he entered the inn. "I am very hungry, and should be glad if you would roast this cock for me as soon as possible. *This* cock and no other—mind what I say," he went on. "Oh, and another thing! You can light the fire with this basket. When you have done that I will show you something I have in my bag," and, as he spoke, he tried to imitate the smile that the Holy Man had given *him*.

These directions made the innkeeper's wife very uneasy. However, she said nothing, and began to roast the cock, while her husband did his best to make the man sleepy with wine, but all in vain.

After dinner, which he did not eat without grumbling, for the cock was very tough, the man struck his hand on the table, and said: "Now listen to me. Go and fetch my cock and my basket, at once. Do you hear?"

"Your cock, and your basket, Father Grumbler? But you have just—"

"My cock and *my* basket!" interrupted he. "And, if you are too deaf and too stupid to understand what that means, I have got something which may help to teach you." And opening the bag he cried: "Flack! flick! switch, be quick."

And flack! flick! like lightning a white switch sprang out of the bag and gave such hearty blows to the innkeeper and his wife, and to Father Grumbler into the bargain, that they all jumped as high as feathers when a mattress is shaken.

"Stop! stop! make it stop, and you shall have back your cock and basket," cried the man and his wife. And Father Grumbler, who had no wish to go on, called out between his hops: "Stop then, can't you? That is enough for today!"

But the switch paid no attention, and dealt out its blows as before, and *might* have been dealing them to this day, if the Holy Man had not heard their cries and come to the rescue. "Into the bag, quick," said he, and the switch obeyed.

"Now go and fetch me the cock and the basket," and the woman went without a word, and placed them on the table.

"You have all got what you deserved," continued the Holy Man, "and I have no pity for any of you. I shall take my treasures home, and perhaps some day I may find a man who knows how to make the best of the chances that are given him. But that will never be *you*," he added, turning to Father Grumbler.

Jack and the Beanstalk

❦

ONCE UPON A TIME there was a poor widow who lived in a little cottage with her only son Jack.

Jack was a giddy, thoughtless boy, but very kind-hearted and affectionate. There had been a hard winter, and after it the poor woman had suffered from fever and ague. Jack did no work as yet, and by degrees they grew dreadfully poor. The widow saw that there was no means of keeping Jack and herself from starvation but by selling her cow; so one morning she said to her son, "I am too weak to go myself, Jack, so you must take the cow to market for me, and sell her."

Jack liked going to market to sell the cow very much; but as he was on the way, he met a butcher who had some beautiful beans in his hand. Jack stopped to look at them, and the butcher told the boy that they were of great value, and persuaded the silly lad to sell the cow for these beans.

When he brought them home to his mother instead of the money she expected for her nice cow, she was very vexed and shed many tears, scolding Jack for his folly. He was very sorry, and mother and son went to bed very sad that night; their last hope seemed gone.

At daybreak Jack rose and went out into the garden.

"At least," he thought, "I will sow the wonderful beans. Mother says that they are just common scarlet-runners, and nothing else; but I may as well sow them."

192

So he took a piece of stick, and made some holes in the ground, and put in the beans.

That day they had very little dinner, and went sadly to bed, knowing that for the next day there would be none and Jack, unable to sleep from grief and vexation, got up at day-dawn and went out into the garden.

What was his amazement to find that the beans had grown up in the night, and climbed up and up till they covered the high cliff that sheltered the cottage, and disappeared above it! The stalks had twined and twisted themselves together till they formed quite a ladder.

"It would be easy to climb it," thought Jack.

And, having thought of the experiment, he at once resolved to carry it out, for Jack was a good climber. However, after his late mistake about the cow, he thought he had better consult his mother first.

So Jack called his mother, and they both gazed in silent wonder at the Beanstalk, which was not only of great height, but was thick enough to bear Jack's weight.

"I wonder where it ends," said Jack to his mother; "I think I will climb up and see."

His mother wished him not to venture up this strange ladder, but Jack coaxed her to give her consent to the attempt, for he was certain there must be something wonderful in the Beanstalk; so at last she yielded to his wishes.

Jack instantly began to climb, and went up and up on the ladderlike bean till everything he had left behind him—the cottage, the village, and even the tall church tower—looked quite little, and still he could not see the top of the Beanstalk.

Jack felt a little tired, and thought for a moment that he would go back again; but he was a very persevering boy, and he knew that the way to succeed in anything is not to give up. So after resting for a moment he went on.

After climbing higher and higher, till he grew afraid to look down for fear he should be giddy, Jack at last reached the top of the Beanstalk, and found himself in a beautiful country, finely wooded, with beautiful meadows covered with sheep. A crystal stream ran through the pastures; not far from the place where he had got off the Beanstalk stood a fine, strong castle.

Jack wondered very much that he had never heard of or seen this castle before; but when he reflected on the subject, he saw that it was as much separated from the village by the perpendicular rock on which it stood as if it were in another land.

While Jack was standing looking at the castle, a very strange-looking woman came out of the wood, and advanced toward him.

She wore a pointed cap of quilted red satin turned up with ermine, her hair streamed loose over her shoulders, and she walked with a staff. Jack took off his cap and made her a bow.

"If you please, ma'am," said he, "is this your house?"

"No," said the old lady. "Listen, and I will tell you the story of that castle.

"Once upon a time there was a noble knight, who lived in this castle, which is on the borders of Fairyland. He had a fair and beloved wife and several lovely children: and as his neighbors, the little people, were very friendly toward him, they bestowed on him many excellent and precious gifts.

"Rumor whispered of these treasures; and a monstrous giant, who lived at no great distance, and who was a very wicked being, resolved to obtain possession of them.

"So he bribed a false servant to let him inside the castle, when the knight was in bed and asleep, and he killed him as he lay. Then he went to the part of the castle which was the nursery, and also killed all the poor little ones he found there.

"Happily for her, the lady was not to be found. She had gone with her infant son, who was only two or three months old, to visit her old nurse, who lived in the valley; and she had been detained all night there by a storm.

The next morning, as soon as it was light, one of the servants at the castle, who had managed to escape, came to tell the poor lady of the sad fate of her husband and her pretty babes. She could scarcely believe him at first, and was eager at once to go back and share the fate of her dear ones; but the old nurse, with many tears, besought her to remember that she had still a child, and that it was her duty to preserve her life for the sake of the poor innocent.

"The lady yielded to this reasoning, and consented to remain at her nurse's house as the best place of concealment; for the servant told her that the giant had vowed, if he could find her, he would kill both her and her baby. Years rolled on. The old nurse died, leaving her cottage and the few articles of furniture it contained to her poor lady, who dwelt in it, working as a peasant for her daily bread. Her spinning wheel and the milk of a cow, which she had purchased with the little money she had with her, sufficed for the scanty subsistence of herself and her little son. There was a nice little garden attached to the cottage, in which they cultivated peas, beans, and cabbages, and the lady was not ashamed to go out at harvest time, and glean in the fields to supply her little son's wants.

"Jack, that poor lady is your mother. This castle was once your father's, and must again be yours."

Jack uttered a cry of surprise.

"My mother! Oh, madam, what ought I to do? My poor father! My dear mother!"

"Your duty requires you to win it back for your mother. But the task is a very difficult one, and full of peril, Jack. Have you courage to undertake it?"

"I fear nothing when I am doing right," said Jack.

"Then," said the lady in the red cap, "you are one of those who slay giants. You must get into the castle, and if possible possess yourself of a hen that lays golden eggs, and a harp that talks. Remember, all the giant possesses is really yours." As she ceased speaking, the lady of the red hat suddenly disappeared, and of course Jack knew she was a fairy.

Jack determined at once to attempt the adventure; so he advanced, and blew the horn which hung at the castle portal. The door was opened in a minute or two by a frightful giantess, with one great eye in the middle of her forehead.

As soon as Jack saw her he turned to run away, but she caught him, and dragged him into the castle.

"Ho, ho!" she laughed terribly. "You didn't expect to see *me* here, that is clear! No, I shan't let you go again. I am weary of my life. I am so overworked, and I don't see why I should not have a page as well as other ladies. And you shall be my boy. You shall clean the knives, and black the boots, and make the fires, and help me generally when the giant is out. When he is at home I must hide you, for he has eaten up all my pages hitherto, and you would be a dainty morsel, my little lad."

While she spoke she dragged Jack right into the castle. The poor boy was very much frightened, as I am sure you and I would have been in his place. But he remembered that fear disgraces a man; so he struggled to be brave and make the best of things.

"I am quite ready to help you, and do all I can to serve you, madam," he said, "only I beg you will be good enough to hide me from your husband, for I should not like to be eaten at all."

"That's a good boy," said the Giantess, nodding her head; "it is lucky for you that you did not scream out when you saw me, as the other boys who have been here did, for if you had done so my husband would have awakened and have eaten you, as he did them, for breakfast. Come here, child; go into my wardrobe: he never ventures to open *that*; you will be safe there."

And she opened a huge wardrobe which stood in the great hall, and shut him into it. But the keyhole was so large that it admitted plenty of air, and he could see everything that took place through it. By-and-by he heard a heavy tramp on the stairs, like the lumbering along of a great cannon, and then a voice like thunder cried out:

> *"Fe, fa, fi-fo-fum,*
> *I smell the breath of an Englishman.*
> *Let him be alive or let him be dead,*
> *I'll grind his bones to make my bread."*

"Wife," cried the Giant, "there is a man in the castle. Let me have him for breakfast."

"You are grown old and stupid," cried the lady in her loud tones. "It is only a nice fresh steak off an elephant, that I have cooked for you, which you smell. There, sit down and make a good breakfast."

And she placed a huge dish before him of savory steaming meat, which greatly pleased him, and made him forget his idea of an Englishman being in the castle. When he had breakfasted he went out for a walk; and then the Giantess opened the door, and made Jack come out to help her. He helped her all day. She fed him well, and when evening came put him back in the wardrobe.

The Giant came in to supper. Jack watched him through the keyhole, and was amazed to see him pick a wolf's bone, and put half a fowl at a time into his capacious mouth.

When the supper was ended he bade his wife bring him his hen that laid the golden eggs.

"It lays as well as it did when it belonged to that paltry knight," he said; "indeed I think the eggs are heavier than ever."

The Giantess went away, and soon returned with a little brown hen, which she placed on the table before her husband. "And now, my dear," she said, "I am going for a walk, if you don't want me any longer."

"Go," said the Giant; "I shall be glad to have a nap by-and-by."

Then he took up the brown hen and said to her:

"Lay!" And she instantly laid a golden egg.

"Lay!" said the Giant again. And she laid another.

"Lay!" he repeated the third time. And again a golden egg lay on the table.

Now Jack was sure this hen was that of which the fairy had spoken.

Jack and the Beanstalk

By-and-by the Giant put the hen down on the floor, and soon after went fast asleep, snoring so loud that it sounded like thunder.

Directly Jack perceived that the Giant was fast asleep, he pushed open the door of the wardrobe and crept out; very softly he stole across the room, and, picking up the hen, made haste to quit the apartment. He knew the way to the kitchen, the door of which he found was left ajar; he opened it, shut and locked it after him, and flew back to the Beanstalk, which he descended as fast as his feet would move.

When his mother saw him enter the house she wept for joy, for she had feared that the fairies had carried him away, or that the Giant had found him. But Jack put the brown hen down before her, and told her how he had been in the Giant's castle, and all his adventures. She was very glad to see the hen, which would make them rich once more.

Jack made another journey up the Beanstalk to the Giant's castle one day while his mother had gone to market; but first he dyed his hair and disguised himself. The old woman did not know him again, and dragged him in as she had done before, to help her to do the work; but she heard her husband coming, and hid him in the wardrobe, not thinking that it was the same boy who had stolen the hen. She bade him stay quite still there, or the Giant would eat him.

Then the Giant came in saying:

> "Fe, fa, fi-fo-fum,
> I smell the breath of an Englishman.
> Let him be alive or let him be dead,
> I'll grind his bones to make my bread."

"Nonsense!" said the wife, "it is only a roasted bullock that I thought would be a tidbit for your supper; sit down and I will bring it up at once." The Giant sat down, and soon his wife brought up a roasted bullock on a large dish, and they began their supper. Jack was amazed to see them pick the bones of the bullock as if it had been a lark. As soon as they had finished their meal, the Giantess rose and said:

"Now, my dear, with your leave I am going up to my room to finish the story I am reading. If you want me call for me."

"First," answered the Giant, "bring me my money bags, that I may count my golden pieces before I sleep." The Giantess obeyed. She went and soon returned with two large bags over her shoulders, which she put down by her husband.

"There," she said; "that is all that is left of the knight's money. When you have spent it you must go and take another baron's castle."

"That he shan't, if I can help it," thought Jack.

The Giant, when his wife was gone, took out heaps and heaps of golden pieces, and counted them, and put them in piles, till he was tired of the amusement. Then he swept them all back into their bags, and leaning back in his chair fell fast asleep, snoring so loud that no other sound was audible.

Jack stole softly out of the wardrobe, and taking up the bags of money (which were his very own, because the Giant had stolen them from his father), he ran off, and with great difficulty descending the Beanstalk, laid the bags of gold on his mother's table. She had just returned from town, and was crying at not finding Jack.

"There, mother, I have brought you the gold that my father lost."

"Oh, Jack! you are a very good boy, but I wish you would not risk your precious life in the Giant's castle. Tell me how you came to go there again."

And Jack told her all about it.

Jack's mother was very glad to get the money, but she did not like him to run any risk for her.

But after a time Jack made up his mind to go again to the Giant's castle.

So he climbed the Beanstalk once more, and blew the horn at the Giant's gate. The Giantess soon opened the door; she was very stupid, and did not know him again, but she stopped a minute before she took him in. She feared another robbery; but Jack's fresh face looked so innocent that she could not resist him, and so she bade him come in, and again hid him away in the wardrobe.

By-and-by the Giant came home, and as soon as he had crossed the threshold he roared out:

"Fe, fa, fi-fo-fum,
I smell the breath of an Englishman.
Let him be alive or let him be dead,
I'll grind his bones to make my bread."

"You stupid old Giant," said his wife, "you only smell a nice sheep, which I have grilled for your dinner."

And the Giant sat down, and his wife brought up a whole sheep for his dinner. When he had eaten it all up, he said:

"Now bring me my harp, and I will have a little music while you take your walk."

The Giantess obeyed, and returned with a beautiful harp. The framework was all sparkling with diamonds and rubies, and the strings were all of gold.

"This is one of the nicest things I took from the knight," said the Giant. "I am very fond of music, and my harp is a faithful servant."

So he drew the harp toward him, and said:

"Play!"

And the harp played a very soft, sad air.

"Play something merrier!" said the Giant.

And the harp played a merry tune.

"Now play me a lullaby," roared the Giant; and the harp played a sweet lullaby, to the sound of which its master fell asleep.

Then Jack stole softly out of the wardrobe, and went into the huge kitchen to see if the Giantess had gone out; he found no one there, so he went to the door and opened it softly, for he thought he could not do so with the harp in his hand.

Then he entered the Giant's room and seized the harp and ran away with it; but as he jumped over the threshold the harp called out:

"MASTER! MASTER!"

And the Giant woke up.

With a tremendous roar he sprang from his seat, and in two strides had reached the door.

But Jack was very nimble. He fled like lightning with the harp, talking to it as he went (for he saw it was a fairy), and telling it he was the son of its old master, the knight.

Still the Giant came on so fast that he was quite close to poor Jack, and had stretched out his great hand to catch him. But, luckily, just at that moment he stepped upon a loose stone, stumbled, and fell flat on the ground, where he lay at his full length.

This accident gave Jack time to get on the Beanstalk and hasten down it; but just as he reached their own garden he beheld the Giant descending after him.

"Mother! mother!" cried Jack, "make haste and give me the axe."

His mother ran to him with a hatchet in her hand, and Jack with

one tremen-
dous blow cut
through all the
Beanstalks except
one.

"Now, mother,
stand out of the way!"
said he.

Jack's mother shrank back, and
it was well she did so, for just as the
Giant took hold of the last branch of the Beanstalk, Jack cut the stem
quite through and darted from the spot.

Down came the Giant with a terrible crash, and as he fell on his
head, he broke his neck, and lay dead at the feet of the woman he had
so much injured.

Before Jack and his mother had recovered from their alarm and
agitation, a beautiful lady stood before them.

"Jack," said she, "you have acted like a brave knight's son, and
deserve to have your inheritance restored to you. Dig a grave and bury
the Giant, and then go and kill the Giantess."

"But," said Jack, "I could not kill anyone unless I were fighting with
him; and I could not draw my sword upon a woman. Moreover, the
Giantess was very kind to me."

Jack and the Beanstalk

The Fairy smiled on Jack.

"I am very much pleased with your generous feeling," she said. "Nevertheless, return to the castle, and act as you will find needful."

Jack asked the Fairy if she would show him the way to the castle, as the Beanstalk was now down. She told him that she would drive him there in her chariot, which was drawn by two peacocks. Jack thanked her, and sat down in the chariot with her.

The Fairy drove him a long distance around, till they reached a village which lay at the bottom of the hill. Here they found a number of miserable-looking men assembled. The Fairy stopped her carriage and addressed them:

"My friends," said she, "the cruel giant who oppressed you and ate up all your flocks and herds is dead, and this young gentleman was the means of your being delivered from him, and is the son of your kind old master, the knight."

The men gave a loud cheer at these words, and pressed forward to say that they would serve Jack as faithfully as they had served his father. The Fairy bade them follow her to the castle, and they marched thither in a body, and Jack blew the horn and demanded admittance.

The old Giantess saw them coming from the turret loop-hole. She was very much frightened, for she guessed that something had happened to her husband; and as she came downstairs very fast she caught her foot in her dress, and fell from the top to the bottom and broke her neck.

When the people outside found that the door was not opened to them, they took crowbars and forced the portal. Nobody was to be seen, but on leaving the hall they found the body of the Giantess at the foot of the stairs.

Thus Jack took possession of the castle. The Fairy went and brought his mother to him, with the hen and the harp. He had the Giantess buried, and endeavored as much as lay in his power to do right to those whom the Giant had robbed.

Before her departure for fairyland, the Fairy explained to Jack that she had sent the butcher to meet him with the beans, in order to try what sort of lad he was.

"If you had looked at the gigantic Beanstalk and only stupidly wondered about it," she said, "I should have left you where misfortune had placed you, only restoring her cow to your mother. But you showed an inquiring mind, and great courage and enterprise, therefore you deserve to rise; and when you mounted the Beanstalk you climbed the Ladder of Fortune."

She then took her leave of Jack and his mother.

Snowdrop

Once upon a time, in the middle of winter when the snowflakes were falling like feathers on the earth, a Queen sat at a window framed in black ebony and sewed. And as she sewed and gazed out to the white landscape, she pricked her finger with the needle, and three drops of blood fell on the snow outside, and because the red showed out so well against the white she thought to herself:

"Oh! what wouldn't I give to have a child as white as snow, as red as blood, and as black as ebony!"

And her wish was granted, for not long after a little daughter was born to her, with skin as white as snow, lips and cheeks as red as blood, and hair as black as ebony. They called her Snowdrop, and not long after her birth the Queen died.

After a year the King married again. His new wife was a beautiful woman, but so proud and overbearing that she couldn't stand any rival to her beauty. She possessed a magic mirror, and when she used to stand before it gazing at her own reflection and ask:

"Mirror, mirror, hanging there,
Who in all the land's most fair?"

it always replied:

Snowdrop

"You are most fair, my Lady Queen,
None fairer in the land, I ween."

Then she was quite happy, for she knew the mirror always spoke the truth.

But Snowdrop was growing prettier and prettier every day, and when she was seven years old she was as beautiful as she could be, and fairer even than the Queen herself. One day when the latter asked her mirror the usual question, it replied:

"My Lady Queen, you are fair, 'tis true,
But Snowdrop is fairer far than you."

Then the Queen flew into the most awful passion, and turned every shade of green in her jealousy. From this hour she hated poor Snowdrop like poison, and every day her envy, hatred, and malice grew, for envy and jealousy are like evil weeds which spring up and choke the heart.

At last she could endure Snowdrop's presence no longer, and, calling a huntsman to her, she said:

"Take the child out into the wood, and never let me see her face again. You must kill her, and bring me back her lungs and liver, that I may know for certain she is dead."

The Huntsman did as he was told and led Snowdrop out into the wood, but as he was in the act of drawing out his knife to slay her, she began to cry, and said:

"Oh, dear Huntsman, spare my life, and I will promise to fly forth into the wide wood and never to return home again."

And because she was so young and pretty the Huntsman had pity on her, and said:

"Well, run along, poor child." For he thought to himself: "The wild beasts will soon eat her up."

And his heart felt lighter because he hadn't had to do the deed himself. And as he turned away a young boar came running past, so he shot it, and brought its lungs and liver home to the Queen as a proof that Snowdrop was really dead. And the wicked woman had them stewed in salt, and ate them up, thinking she had made an end of Snowdrop for ever.

Now when the poor child found herself alone in the big wood the very trees around her seemed to assume strange shapes, and she felt so frightened she didn't know what to do. Then she began to run over the sharp stones, and through the bramble bushes, and the wild beasts ran past her, but they did her no harm. She ran as far as her legs would carry her, and as evening approached she saw a little house, and she stepped inside to rest. Everything was very small in the little house, but cleaner and neater than anything you can imagine. In the middle of the room there stood a little table, covered with a white tablecloth, and

seven little plates and forks and spoons and knives and tumblers. Side by side against the wall there were seven little beds, covered with snow-white counterpanes. Snowdrop felt so hungry and so thirsty that she ate a bit of bread and a little porridge from each plate, and drank a drop of wine out of each tumbler. Then feeling tired and sleepy she lay down on one of the beds, but it wasn't comfortable; then she tried all the others in turn, but one was too long, and another too short, and it was only when she got to the seventh that she found one to suit her exactly. So she lay down upon it, said her prayers like a good child, and fell fast asleep.

When it got quite dark the masters of the little house returned. They were seven Dwarfs who worked in the mines, right down deep in the heart of the mountain. They lighted their seven little lamps, and as soon as their eyes got accustomed to the glare they saw that someone had been in the room, for all was not in the same order as they had left it.

The first said:

"Who's been sitting on my little chair?"

The second said:

"Who's been eating my little loaf?"

The third said:

"Who's been tasting my porridge?"

The fourth said:

"Who's been eating out of my little plate?"

The fifth said:

"Who's been using my little fork?"

The sixth said:

"Who's been cutting with my little knife?"

The seventh said:

"Who's been drinking out of my little tumbler?"

Then the first Dwarf looked around and saw a little hollow in his bed, and he asked again:

"Who's been lying on my bed?"

The others came running around, and cried when they saw their beds:

"Somebody has lain on ours too."

But when the seventh came to his bed, he started back in amazement, for there he beheld Snowdrop fast asleep. Then he called the others, who turned their little lamps full on the bed, and when they saw Snowdrop lying there they nearly fell down with surprise.

"Goodness gracious!" they cried, "what a beautiful child!"

And they were so enchanted by her beauty that they did not wake her, but let her sleep on in the little bed. But the seventh Dwarf slept with his companions one hour in each bed, and in this way he managed to pass the night.

Snowdrop

In the morning Snowdrop awoke, but when she saw the seven little Dwarfs she felt very frightened. But they were so friendly and asked her what her name was in such a kind way, that she replied:

"I am Snowdrop."

"Why did you come to our house?" continued the Dwarfs.

Then she told them how her stepmother had wished her put to death, and how the Huntsman had spared her life, and how she had run the whole day till she had come to their little house. The Dwarfs, when they had heard her sad story, asked her:

"Will you stay and keep house for us, cook, make the beds, do the washing, sew and knit? And if you give satisfaction and keep everything neat and clean, you shall want for nothing."

"Yes," answered Snowdrop, "I will gladly do all you ask."

And so she took up her abode with them. Every morning the Dwarfs went into the mountain to dig for gold, and in the evening, when they returned home, Snowdrop always had their supper ready for them. But during the day the girl was left quite alone, so the good Dwarfs warned her, saying:

"Beware of your stepmother. She will soon find out you are here, and whatever you do don't let anyone into the house."

Now the Queen, after she thought she had eaten Snowdrop's lungs and liver, never dreamed but that she was once more the most beautiful woman in the world; so stepping before her mirror one day she said:

> "Mirror, mirror, hanging there,
> Who in all the land's most fair?"

and the mirror replied:

Snowdrop

"My Lady Queen, you are fair, 'tis true,
But Snowdrop is fairer far than you.
Snowdrop, who dwells with the seven little men,
Is as fair as you, as fair again."

When the Queen heard these words she was nearly struck dumb with horror, for the mirror always spoke the truth, and she knew now that the Huntsman must have deceived her, and that Snowdrop was still alive. She pondered day and night how she might destroy her, for as long as she felt she had a rival in the land her jealous heart left her no rest. At last she hit upon a plan. She stained her face and dressed herself up as an old peddler wife, so that she was quite unrecognizable. In this guise she went over the seven hills till she came to the house of the seven Dwarfs. There she knocked at the door, calling out at the same time:

"Fine wares to sell, fine wares to sell!"

Snowdrop peeped out of the window, and called out:

"Good-day, mother, what have you to sell?"

"Good wares, fine wares," she answered; "laces of every shade and description," and she held one up that was made of some gay colored silk.

"Surely I can let the honest woman in," thought Snowdrop; so she unbarred the door and bought the pretty lace.

"Good gracious! child," said the old woman, "what a figure you've got. Come! I'll lace you up properly for once."

Snowdrop, suspecting no evil, stood before her and let her lace her bodice up, but the old woman laced her so quickly and so tightly that it took Snowdrop's breath away, and she fell down dead.

"Now you are no longer the fairest," said the wicked old woman, and then she hastened away.

Snowdrop

In the evening the seven Dwarfs came home, and you may think what a fright they got when they saw their dear Snowdrop lying on the floor, as still and motionless as a dead person. They lifted her up tenderly, and when they saw how tightly laced she was they cut the lace in two, and she began to breathe a little and gradually came back to life. When the Dwarfs heard what had happened, they said:

"Depend upon it, the old peddler wife was none other than the old Queen. In future you must be sure to let no one in, if we are not at home."

As soon as the wicked old Queen got home she went straight to her mirror, and said:

> "Mirror, mirror, hanging there,
> Who in all the land's most fair?"

and the mirror answered as before:

> "My Lady Queen, you are fair, 'tis true,
> But Snowdrop is fairer far than you.
> Snowdrop, who dwells with the seven little men,
> Is as fair as you, as fair again."

When she heard this she became as pale as death, because she saw at once that Snowdrop must be alive again.

"This time," she said to herself, "I will think of something that will make an end of her once and for all."

And by the witchcraft which she understood so well she made a poisonous comb; then she dressed herself up and assumed the form of another old woman. So she went over the seven hills till she reached the house of the seven Dwarfs, and knocking at the door she called out:

"Fine wares for sale."

Snowdrop looked out of the window and said:

"You must go away, for I may not let anyone in."

"But surely you are not forbidden to look out?" said the old woman, and she held up the poisonous comb for her to see.

It pleased the girl so much that she let herself be taken in, and opened the door. When they had settled their bargain the old woman said:

"Now I'll comb your hair properly for you, for once in the way."

Poor Snowdrop thought no evil, but hardly had the comb touched her hair than the poison worked and she fell down unconscious.

"Now, my fine lady, you're really done for this time," said the wicked woman, and she made her way home as fast as she could.

Fortunately it was now near evening, and the seven Dwarfs returned home. When they saw Snowdrop lying dead on the ground, they at once suspected that her wicked stepmother had been at work again; so they searched till they found the poisonous comb, and the moment they pulled it out of her head Snowdrop came to herself again, and told them what had happened. Then they warned her once more to be on her guard, and to open the door to no one.

As soon as the Queen got home she went straight to her mirror, and asked:

> *"Mirror, mirror, hanging there,*
> *Who in all the land's most fair?"*

and it replied as before:

> *"My Lady Queen, you are fair, 'tis true,*
> *But Snowdrop is fairer far than you.*

Snowdrop

Snowdrop, who dwells with the seven little men,
Is as fair as you, as fair again."

When she heard these words she literally trembled and shook with rage.

"Snowdrop shall die," she cried; "yes, though it cost me my own life."

Then she went to a little secret chamber, which no one knew of but herself, and there she made a poisonous apple. Outwardly it looked beautiful, white with red cheeks, so that everyone who saw it longed to eat it, but anyone who might do so would certainly die on the spot. When the apple was quite finished she stained her face and dressed herself up as a peasant, and so she went over the seven hills to the seven Dwarfs'. She knocked at the door, as usual, but Snowdrop put her head out of the window and called out:

"I may not let anyone in, the seven Dwarfs have forbidden me to do so."

"Are you afraid of being poisoned?" asked the old woman. "See, I will cut this apple in half. I'll eat the white cheek and you can eat the red."

But the apple was so cunningly made that only the red cheek was poisonous. Snowdrop longed to eat the tempting fruit, and when she saw that the peasant woman was eating it herself, she couldn't resist the temptation any longer, and stretching out her hand she took the poisonous half. But hardly had the first bite passed her lips than she fell down dead on the ground. Then the eyes of the cruel Queen sparkled with glee, and laughing aloud she cried:

"As white as snow, as red as blood, and as black as ebony, this time the Dwarfs won't be able to bring you back to life."

When she got home she asked the mirror:

Snowdrop

"Mirror, mirror, hanging there,
Who in all the land's most fair?"

and this time it replied:

"You are most fair, my Lady Queen,
None fairer in the land, I ween."

Then her jealous heart was at rest—at least, as much at rest as a jealous heart can ever be.

When the little Dwarfs came home in the evening they found Snowdrop lying on the ground, and she neither breathed nor stirred. They lifted her up, and looked around everywhere to see if they could find anything poisonous about. They unlaced her bodice, combed her hair, washed her with water and wine, but all in vain; the child was dead and remained dead. Then they placed her on a bier, and all the seven Dwarfs sat around it, weeping and sobbing for three whole days. At last they made up their minds to bury her, but she looked as blooming as a living being, and her cheeks were still such a lovely color, that they said:

"We can't hide her away in the black ground."

So they had a coffin made of transparent glass, and they laid her in it, and wrote on the lid in golden letters that she was a royal Princess. Then they put the coffin on the top of the mountain, and one of the Dwarfs always remained beside it and kept watch over it. And the very birds of the air came and bewailed Snowdrop's death, first an owl, and then a raven, and last of all a little dove.

Snowdrop lay a long time in the coffin, and she always looked the same, just as if she were fast asleep, and she remained as white as snow,

as red as blood, and her hair as black as ebony.

Now it happened one day that a Prince came to the wood and passed by the Dwarfs' house. He saw the coffin on the hill, with the beautiful Snowdrop inside it, and when he had read what was written on it in golden letters, he said to the Dwarf:

"Give me the coffin. I'll give you whatever you like for it."

But the Dwarf said: "No; we wouldn't part with it for all the gold in the world."

"Well, then," he replied, "give it to me, because I can't live without Snowdrop. I will cherish and love it as my dearest possession."

He spoke so sadly that the good Dwarfs had pity on him, and gave him the coffin, and the Prince made his servants bear it away on their shoulders. Now it happened that as they were going down the hill they stumbled over a bush, and jolted the coffin so violently that the poisonous bit of apple Snowdrop had swallowed fell out of her throat. She gradually opened her eyes, lifted up the lid of the coffin and sat up alive and well.

"Oh! dear me, where am I?" she cried.

The Prince answered joyfully, "You are with me," and he told her all that had happened, adding, "I love you better than anyone in all the whole wide world. Will you come with me to my father's palace and be my wife?"

Snowdrop consented, and went with him, and the marriage was celebrated with great pomp and splendor.

Now Snowdrop's wicked stepmother was one of the guests invited to the wedding feast. When she had dressed herself very gorgeously for the occasion, she went to the mirror, and said:

> "Mirror, mirror, hanging there,
> Who in all the land's most fair?"

and the mirror answered:

"My Lady Queen, you are fair, 'tis true,
But Snowdrop is fairer far than you."

When the wicked woman heard these words she uttered a curse, and was beside herself with rage and mortification. At first she didn't want to go to the wedding at all, but at the same time she felt she would never be happy till she had seen the young Queen. As she entered Snowdrop recognized her, and nearly fainted with fear; but red-hot iron shoes had been prepared for the wicked old Queen, and she was made to get into them and dance till she fell down dead.

Snow-white and Rose-red

❧

A POOR WIDOW ONCE LIVED in a little cottage with a garden in front of it, in which grew two rose trees, one bearing white roses and the other red. She had two children, who were just like the two rose trees; one was called Snow-white and the other Rose-red, and they were the sweetest and best children in the world, always diligent and always cheerful; but Snow-white was quieter and more gentle than Rose-red. Rose-red loved to run about the fields and meadows, and to pick flowers and catch butterflies; but Snow-white sat at home with her mother and helped her in the household, or read aloud to her when there was no work to do. The two children loved each other so dearly that they always walked about hand-in-hand whenever they went out together, and when Snow-white said: "We will never desert each other," Rose-red answered: "No, not as long as we live"; and the mother added: "Whatever one gets she shall share with the other." They often roamed about in the wood gathering berries and no beast offered to hurt them; on the contrary, they came up to them in the most confiding manner; the little hare would eat a cabbage leaf from their hands, the deer grazed beside them, the stag would bound past them merrily, and the birds remained on the branches and sang to them with all their might. No evil ever befell them; if they tarried late in the wood and night overtook them, they lay down together on the

moss and slept till morning, and their mother knew they were quite safe, and never felt anxious about them. Once, when they had slept the night in the wood and had been wakened by the morning sun, they perceived a beautiful child in a shining white robe sitting close to their resting-place. The figure got up, looked at them kindly, but said nothing, and vanished into the wood. And when they looked around about them they became aware that they had slept quite close to a precipice, over which they would certainly have fallen had they gone on a few steps farther in the darkness. And when they told their mother of their adventure, she said what they had seen must have been the angel that guards good children.

Snow-white and Rose-red kept their mother's cottage so beautifully clean and neat that it was a pleasure to go into it. In summer Rose-red looked after the house, and every morning before her mother awoke she placed a bunch of flowers before the bed, from each tree a rose. In winter Snow-white lit the fire and put on the kettle, which was made of brass, but so beautifully polished that it shone like gold. In the evening when the snowflakes fell their mother said: "Snow-white, go and close the shutters"; and they drew around the fire, while the mother put on her spectacles and read aloud from a big book and the two girls listened and sat and span. Beside them on the ground lay a little lamb, and behind them perched a little white dove with its head tucked under its wings.

One evening as they sat thus cozily together someone knocked at the door as though he desired admittance. The mother said: "Rose-red, open the door quickly; it must be some traveler seeking shelter." Rose-red hastened to unbar the door, and thought she saw a poor man standing in the darkness outside; but it was no such thing, only a bear, who poked his thick black head through the door. Rose-red screamed aloud and sprang back in terror, the lamb began to bleat, the dove flapped its wings, and Snow-white ran and hid behind her mother's bed. But the bear began to speak, and said: "Don't be afraid: I won't hurt you. I am half frozen, and only wish to warm myself a little." "My poor bear," said the mother, "lie down by the fire, only take care you don't burn your fur." Then she called out: "Snow-white and Rose-red, come out; the bear will do you no harm: he is a good, honest creature." So they both came out of their hiding places, and gradually the lamb and dove drew near too, and they all forgot their fear. The bear asked the children to beat the snow a little out of his fur, and they fetched a brush and scrubbed him till he was dry. Then the beast stretched himself in front of the fire, and growled quite happily and comfortably. The children soon grew quite at their ease with him, and led their helpless guest a fearful life. They tugged his fur with their hands, put their small feet on his back, and rolled him about here and there, or took a hazel wand and beat him with it; and if he growled they only laughed. The bear submitted to everything with the best possible good nature, only when they went too far he cried: "Oh! children, spare my life!

> *Snow-white and Rose-red,*
> *Don't beat your lover dead."*

When it was time to retire for the night, and the others went to bed, the mother said to the bear: "You can lie there on the hearth, in heaven's name; it will be shelter for you from the cold and wet." As soon as day dawned the children let him out, and he trotted over the snow into the wood. From this time on the bear came every evening at the same hour, and lay down by the hearth and let the children play what pranks they liked with him; and they got so accustomed to him that the door was never shut till their black friend had made his appearance.

When spring came, and all outside was green, the bear said one morning to Snow-white: "Now I must go away, and not return again the whole summer." "Where are you going to, dear bear?" asked Snow-white. "I must go to the wood and protect my treasure from the wicked dwarfs. In winter, when the earth is frozen hard, they are obliged to remain underground, for they can't work their way through; but now, when the sun has thawed and warmed the ground, they break through and come up above to spy the land and steal what they can: what once falls into their hands and into their caves is not easily brought back to light." Snow-white was quite sad over their friend's departure, and when she unbarred the door for him, the bear, stepping out, caught a piece of his fur in the doorknocker, and Snow-white thought she caught sight of glittering gold beneath it, but she couldn't be certain of it; and the bear ran hastily away, and soon disappeared behind the trees.

Snow-white and Rose-red

A short time after this the mother sent the children into the wood to collect fagots. They came in their wanderings upon a big tree which lay felled on the ground, and on the trunk among the long grass they noticed something jumping up and down, but what it was they couldn't distinguish. When they approached nearer they perceived a dwarf with a wizened face and a beard a yard long. The end of the beard was jammed into a cleft of the tree, and the little man sprang about like a dog on a chain, and didn't seem to know what he was to do. He glared at the girls with his fiery red eyes, and screamed out: "What are you standing there for? Can't you come and help me?" "What were you doing, little man?" asked Rose-red. "You stupid, inquisitive goose!" replied the dwarf; "I wanted to split the tree, in order to get little chips of wood for our kitchen fire; those thick logs that serve to make fires for coarse, greedy people like yourselves quite burn up all the little food we need. I had successfully driven in the wedge, and all was going well, but the cursed wood was so slippery that it suddenly sprang out, and the tree closed up so rapidly that I had no time to take my beautiful white beard out, so here I am stuck fast, and I can't get away; and you silly, smooth-faced, milk-and-water girls just stand and laugh! Ugh! what wretches you are!"

The children did all in their power, but they couldn't get the beard out; it was wedged in far too firmly. "I will run and fetch somebody," said Rose-red. "Crazy blockheads!" snapped the dwarf; "what's the good of calling anyone else? You're already two too many for me. Does nothing better occur to you than that?" "Don't be so impatient," said Snow-white, "I'll see you get help"; and taking her scissors out of her pocket she cut the end off his beard. As soon as the dwarf felt himself free he seized a bag full of gold which was hidden among the roots of the tree, lifted it up, and muttered aloud: "Curse these rude wretches, cutting off a piece of my splendid beard!" With these words he swung the bag over his back, and disappeared without as much as looking at the children again.

Shortly after this Snow-white and Rose-red went out to get a dish of fish. As they approached the stream they saw something which looked like an enormous grasshopper, springing toward the water as if it were going to jump in. They ran forward and recognized their old friend the dwarf. "Where are you going to?" asked Rose-red; "you're surely not going to jump into the water?" "I'm not such a fool," screamed the dwarf. "Don't you see that cursed fish is trying to drag me in?" The little man had been sitting on the bank fishing, when unfortunately the wind had entangled his beard in the line; and when immediately afterward a big fish bit, the feeble little creature had no strength to pull it out; the fish had the upper fin, and dragged the dwarf toward him. He clung on with all his might to every rush and blade of grass, but it didn't help him much; he had to follow every movement of the fish, and was in great danger of being drawn into the water. The girls came up just at the right moment, held him firm, and did all they could to disentangle his beard from the line; but in vain, beard and line were in a hopeless muddle. Nothing remained but to produce the scissors and cut the beard, by which a small part of it was sacrificed.

When the dwarf perceived what they were about he yelled to them: "Do you call that manners, you toadstools! to disfigure a fellow's face? It wasn't enough that you shortened my beard before, but you must now needs cut off the best bit of it. I can't appear like this before my own people. I wish you'd been at Jericho first." Then he fetched a sack of pearls that lay among the rushes, and without saying another word he dragged it away and disappeared behind a stone.

It happened that soon after this the mother sent the two girls to the town to buy needles, thread, laces, and ribbons. Their road led over a heath where huge boulders of rock lay scattered here and there. While trudging along they saw a big bird hovering in the air, circling slowly above them, but always descending lower, till at last it settled on a rock not far from them. Immediately afterward they heard a sharp, piercing cry. They ran forward, and saw with horror that the eagle had pounced on their old friend the dwarf, and was about to carry him off. The tender-hearted children seized a hold of the little man, and struggled so long with the bird that at last he let go his prey. When the dwarf had recovered from the first shock he screamed in his screeching voice: "Couldn't you have treated me more carefully? You have torn my thin little coat all to shreds, useless, awkward hussies that you are!" Then he took a bag of precious stones and vanished under the rocks into his cave. The girls were accustomed to his ingratitude, and went on their way and did their business in town. On their way home, as they were again passing the heath, they surprised the dwarf pouring out his precious stones on an open space, for he had thought no one would pass by at so late an hour. The evening sun shone on the glittering stones, and they glanced and gleamed so beautifully that the children stood still and gazed on them. "What are you standing there gaping for?" screamed the dwarf, and his ashen-gray face became scarlet with rage. He was about to go off with these angry words when a sudden growl was heard, and a black bear trotted out of the wood. The dwarf jumped up in a great fright, but he hadn't time to reach his place of retreat, for the bear was already close to him. Then he cried in terror: "Dear Mr. Bear, spare me! I'll give you all my treasure. Look at those beautiful precious stones lying there. Spare my life! What pleasure would you get from a poor feeble little fellow like me? You won't feel me between your teeth. There, lay hold of these two wicked girls, they will be a tender morsel for you, as fat as young quails; eat them up, for heaven's sake." But the bear, paying no attention to his words, gave the evil little creature one blow with his paw, and he never moved again.

The girls had run away, but the bear called after them: "Snow-white and Rose-red, don't be afraid; wait, and I'll come with you." Then they recognized his voice and stood still, and when the bear was quite close to them his skin suddenly fell off, and a beautiful man stood beside them, all dressed in gold. "I am a king's son," he said, "and have been doomed by that unholy little dwarf, who had stolen my treasure, to roam about the wood as a wild bear till his death should set me free. Now he has got his well-merited punishment."

Snow-white married him, and Rose-red his brother, and they divided the great treasure the dwarf had collected in his cave between them. The old mother lived for many years peacefully with her children; and she carried the two rose trees with her, and they stood in front of her window, and every year they bore the finest red and white roses.

The Tinderbox

A SOLDIER CAME MARCHING along the high road—left, right! left, right! He had his knapsack on his back and a sword by his side, for he had been to the wars and was now returning home.

An old witch met him on the road. She was very ugly to look at: her underlip hung down to her breast.

"Good evening, Soldier!" she said. "What a fine sword and knapsack you have! You are something like a soldier! You ought to have as much money as you would like to carry!"

"Thank you, old Witch," said the Soldier.

"Do you see that great tree there?" said the Witch, pointing to a tree beside them. "It is hollow within. You must climb up to the top, and then you will see a hole through which you can let yourself down into the tree. I will tie a rope around your waist, so that I may be able to pull you up again when you call."

"What shall I do down there?" asked the Soldier.

"Get money!" answered the Witch. "Listen! When you reach the bottom of the tree you will find yourself in a large hall; it is light there, for there are more than three hundred lamps burning. Then you will see three doors, which you can open—the keys are in the locks. If you go into the first room, you will see a great chest in the middle of the floor with a dog sitting upon it; he has eyes as large as saucers, but you needn't trouble about him. I will give you my blue-check apron, which

you must spread out on the floor, and then go back quickly and fetch the dog and set him upon it; open the chest and take as much money as you like. It is copper there. If you would rather have silver, you must go into the next room, where there is a dog with eyes as large as mill wheels. But don't take any notice of him; just set him upon my apron, and help yourself to the money. If you prefer gold, you can get that too, if you go into the third room, and as much as you like to carry. But the dog that guards the chest there has eyes as large as the Round Tower at Copenhagen! He is a savage dog, I can tell you; but you needn't be afraid of him either. Only, put him on my apron and he won't touch you, and you can take out of the chest as much gold as you like!"

"Come, this is not bad!" said the Soldier. "But what am I to give you, old Witch; for surely you are not going to do this for nothing?"

"Yes, I am!" replied the Witch. "Not a single farthing will I take! For me you shall bring nothing but an old tinderbox which my grandmother forgot last time she was down there."

"Well, tie the rope around my waist!" said the Soldier.

"Here it is," said the Witch, "and here is my blue-check apron."

Then the Soldier climbed up the tree, let himself down through the hole, and found himself standing, as the Witch had said, underground in the large hall, where the three hundred lamps were burning.

Well, he opened the first door. Ugh! there sat the dog with eyes as big as saucers glaring at him.

"You are a fine fellow!" said the Soldier, and put him on the Witch's apron, took as much copper as his pockets could hold; then he shut the chest, put the dog on it again, and went into the second room. Sure enough there sat the dog with eyes as large as mill wheels.

"You had better not look at me so hard!" said the Soldier. "Your eyes will come out of their sockets!"

And then he set the dog on the apron. When he saw all the silver in the chest, he threw away the copper he had taken, and filled his pockets and knapsack with nothing but silver.

Then he went into the third room. Horrors! the dog there had two eyes, each as large as the Round Tower at Copenhagen, spinning around in his head like wheels.

"Good evening!" said the Soldier and saluted, for he had never seen a dog like this before. But when he had examined him more closely, he thought to himself: "Now then, I've had enough of this!" and put him down on the floor, and opened the chest. Heavens! what a heap of gold there was! With all that he could buy up the whole town, and all the sugar pigs, all the tin soldiers, whips and rockinghorses in the whole world. Now he threw away all the silver with which he had filled his pockets and knapsack, and filled them with gold instead—yes, all his pockets, his knapsack, cap and boots even, so that he could hardly walk. Now he was rich indeed. He put the dog back upon the chest, shut the door, and then called up through the tree:

"Now pull me up again, old Witch!"

"Have you got the tinderbox also?" asked the Witch.

"Botheration!" said the Soldier, "I had clean forgotten it!" And then he went back and fetched it.

The Witch pulled him up, and there he stood again on the high road, with pockets, knapsack, cap and boots filled with gold.

"What do you want to do with the tinderbox?" asked the Soldier.

"That doesn't matter to you," replied the Witch. "You have got your money, give me my tinderbox."

"We'll see!" said the Soldier. "Tell me at once what you want to do with it, or I will draw my sword, and cut off your head!"

"No!" screamed the Witch.

The Soldier immediately cut off her head. That was the end of her! But he tied up all his gold in her apron, slung it like a bundle over his shoulder, put the tinderbox in his pocket, and set out toward the town.

It was a splendid town! He turned into the finest inn, ordered the best chamber and his favorite dinner; for now that he had so much money he was really rich.

It certainly occurred to the servant who had to clean his boots that they were astonishingly old boots for such a rich lord. But that was because he had not yet bought new ones; next day he appeared in respectable boots and fine clothes. Now, instead of a common soldier he had become a noble lord, and the people told him about all the grand doings of the town and the King, and what a beautiful Princess his daughter was.

"How can one get to see her?" asked the Soldier.

"She is never to be seen at all!" they told him; "she lives in a great copper castle, surrounded by many walls and towers! No one except the King may go in or out, for it is prophesied that she will marry a common soldier, and the King cannot submit to that."

"I should very much like to see her," thought the Soldier; but he could not get permission.

Now he lived very gaily, went to the theater, drove in the King's garden, and gave the poor a great deal of money, which was very nice of him; he had experienced in former times how hard it is not to have a farthing in the world. Now he was rich, wore fine clothes, and made many friends, who all said that he was an excellent man, a real nobleman. And the Soldier liked that. But as he was always spending money, and never made any more, at last the day came when he had nothing left but two shillings, and he had to leave the beautiful rooms in which he had been living, and go into a little attic under the roof, and clean his own boots, and mend them with a darning needle. None of his friends came to visit him there, for there were too many stairs to climb.

It was a dark evening, and he could not even buy a light. But all at once it flashed across him that there was a little end of tinder in the tinderbox, which he had taken from the hollow tree into which the Witch had helped him down. He found the box with the tinder in it; but just as he was kindling a light, and had struck a spark out of the tinderbox, the door burst open, and the dog with eyes as large as saucers, which he had seen down in the tree, stood before him and said:

"What does my lord command?"

"What's the meaning of this?" exclaimed the Soldier. "This is a pretty kind of tinderbox, if I can get whatever I want like this. Get me money!" he cried to the dog, and hey, presto! he was off and back again, holding a great purse full of money in his mouth.

Now the Soldier knew what a capital tinderbox this was. If he rubbed once, the dog that sat on the chest of copper appeared; if he rubbed twice, there came the dog that watched over the silver chest; and if he rubbed three times, the one that guarded the gold appeared. Now, the Soldier went down again to his beautiful rooms, and appeared once more in splendid clothes. All his friends immediately recognized him again, and paid him great court.

One day he thought to himself: "It is very strange that no one can get to see the Princess. They all say she is very pretty, but what's the use of that if she has to sit for ever in the great copper castle with all the towers? Can I not manage to see her somehow? Where is my tinderbox?" and so he struck a spark, and, presto! there came the dog with eyes as large as saucers.

"It is the middle of the night, I know," said the Soldier; "but I should very much like to see the Princess for a moment."

The dog was already outside the door, and before the Soldier could look around, in he came with the Princess. She was lying asleep on the dog's back, and was so beautiful that anyone could see she was a real Princess. The Soldier really could not refrain from kissing her—he was such a thorough Soldier. Then the dog ran back with the Princess. But when it was morning, and the King and Queen were drinking tea, the Princess said that the night before she had had such a strange dream about a dog and a soldier: she had ridden on the dog's back, and the Soldier had kissed her.

"That is certainly a fine story," said the Queen. But the next night one of the ladies-in-waiting was to watch at the Princess's bed, to see if it was only a dream, or if it had actually happened.

The Soldier had an overpowering longing to see the Princess again, and so the dog came in the middle of the night and fetched her,

running as fast as he could. But the lady-in-waiting slipped on india rubber shoes and followed them. When she saw them disappear into a large house, she thought to herself: "Now I know where it is"; and made a great cross on the door with a piece of chalk. Then she went home and lay down, and the dog came back also, with the Princess. But when he saw that a cross had been made on the door of the house where the Soldier lived, he took a piece of chalk also, and made crosses on all the doors in the town; and that was very clever, for now the lady-in-waiting could not find the right house, as there were crosses on all the doors.

Early next morning the King, Queen, ladies-in-waiting, and officers came out to see where the Princess had been.

"There it is!" said the King, when he saw the first door with a cross on it.

"No, there it is, my dear!" said the Queen, when she likewise saw a door with a cross.

"But here is one, and there is another!" they all exclaimed; wherever they looked there was a cross on the door. Then they realized that the sign would not help them at all.

But the Queen was an extremely clever woman, who could do a great deal more than just drive in a coach. She took her great golden scissors, cut up a piece of silk, and made a pretty little bag of it. This she filled with the finest buckwheat grains, and tied it around the Princess's neck; this done, she cut a little hole in the bag, so that the grains would strew the whole road wherever the Princess went.

In the night the dog came again, took the Princess on his back and ran away with her to the Soldier, who was very much in love with her, and would have liked to have been a prince, so that he might have had her for his wife.

The dog did not notice how the grains were strewn right from the castle to the Soldier's window, where he ran up the wall with the Princess.

In the morning the King and the Queen saw plainly where their daughter had been, and they took the Soldier and put him into prison.

There he sat. Oh, how dark and dull it was there! And they told him: "Tomorrow you are to be hanged." Hearing that did not exactly cheer him, and he had left his tinderbox in the inn.

Next morning he could see through the iron grating in front of his little window how the people were hurrying out of the town to see him hanged. He heard the drums and saw the soldiers marching; all the people were running to and fro. Just below his window was a shoemaker's apprentice, with leather apron and shoes; he was skipping along so merrily that one of his shoes flew off and fell against the wall, just where the Soldier was sitting peeping through the iron grating.

"Oh, shoemaker's boy, you needn't be in such a hurry!" said the Soldier to him. "There's nothing going on till I arrive. But if you will run back to the house where I lived, and fetch me my tinderbox, I will give you four shillings. But you must put your best foot foremost."

The shoemaker's boy was very willing to earn four shillings, and fetched the tinderbox, gave it to the Soldier, and—yes—now you shall hear.

Outside the town a great scaffold had been erected, and all around were standing the soldiers, and hundreds of thousands of people. The King and Queen were sitting on a magnificent throne opposite the judges and the whole council.

The Soldier was already standing on the top of the ladder; but when they wanted to put the rope around his neck, he said that the fulfillment of one innocent request was always granted to a poor criminal before he underwent his punishment. He would so much like to smoke a small pipe of tobacco; it would be his last pipe in this world.

The King could not refuse him this, and so he took out his tinderbox, and rubbed it once, twice, three times. And lo, and behold! there stood all three dogs—the one with eyes as large as saucers, the second with eyes as large as mill wheels, and the third with eyes each as large as the Round Tower of Copenhagen.

"Help me now, so that I may not be hanged!" cried the Soldier. And thereupon the dogs fell upon the judges and the whole council, seized some by the legs, others by the nose, and threw them so high into the air that they fell and were smashed into pieces.

"I won't stand this!" said the King; but the largest dog seized him too, and the Queen as well, and threw them up after the others. This frightened the soldiers, and all the people cried: "Good Soldier, you shall be our King, and marry the beautiful Princess!"

Then they put the Soldier into the King's coach, and the three dogs danced in front, crying "Hurrah!" And the boys whistled and the soldiers presented arms.

The Princess came out of the copper castle, and became Queen; and that pleased her very much.

The wedding festivities lasted for eight days, and the dogs sat at the table and made eyes at everyone.

The Elf Maiden

ONCE UPON A TIME two young men living in a small village fell in love with the same girl. During the winter, it was all night except for an hour or so about noon, when the darkness seemed a little less dark, and then they used to see which of them could tempt her out for a sleigh ride with the Northern Lights flashing above them, or which could persuade her to come to a dance in some neighboring barn. But when the spring began, and the light grew longer, the hearts of the villagers leaped at the sight of the sun, and a day was fixed for the boats to be brought out, and the great nets to be spread in the bays of some islands that lay a few miles to the north. Everybody went on this expedition, and the two young men and the girl went with them.

They all sailed merrily across the sea chattering like a flock of magpies, or singing their favorite songs. And when they reached the shore, what an unpacking there was! For this was a noted fishing ground, and here they would live, in little wooden huts, till autumn and bad weather came around again.

The maiden and the two young men happened to share the same hut with some friends, and fished daily from the same boat. And as time went on, one of the youths remarked that the girl took less notice of him than she did of his companion. At first he tried to think that he was dreaming, and for a long while he kept his eyes shut very tight to

242

what he did not want to see, but in spite of his efforts, the truth managed to wriggle through, and then the young man gave up trying to deceive himself, and set about finding some way to get the better of his rival.

The plan that he hit upon could not be carried out for some months; but the longer the young man thought of it, the more pleased he was with it, so he made no sign of his feelings, and waited patiently till the moment came. This was the very day that they were all going to leave the islands, and sail back to the mainland for the winter. In the bustle and hurry of departure, the cunning fisherman contrived that their boat should be the last to put off, and when everything was ready, and the sails about to be set, he suddenly called out:

"Oh, dear, what shall I do? I have left my best knife behind in the hut. Run, like a good fellow, and get it for me, while I raise the anchor and loosen the tiller."

Not thinking any harm, the youth jumped back on shore and made his way up the steep bank. At the door of the hut he stopped and looked back, then started and gazed in horror. The head of the boat stood out to sea, and he was left alone on the island.

Yes, there was no doubt of it—he was quite alone; and he had nothing to help him except the knife which his comrade had purposely dropped on the ledge of the window. For some minutes he was too stunned by the treachery of his friend to think about anything at all, but after a while he shook himself awake, and determined that he would manage to keep alive somehow, if it were only to revenge himself.

So he put the knife in his pocket and went off to a part of the island which was not so bare as the rest, and had a small grove of trees. From one of these he cut himself a bow, which he strung with a piece of cord that had been left lying about the huts.

When this was ready the young man ran down to the shore and

shot one or two sea-birds, which he plucked and cooked for supper.

In this way the months slipped by, and Christmas came around again. The evening before, the youth went down to the rocks and into the copse, collecting all the driftwood the sea had washed up or the gale had blown down, and he piled it up in a great stack outside the door, so that he might not have to fetch any all the next day. As soon as his task was done, he paused and looked out toward the mainland, thinking of Christmas Eve last year, and the merry dance they had had. The night was still and cold, and by the help of the Northern Lights he could almost see across to the opposite coast, when, suddenly, he noticed a boat, which seemed steering straight for the island. At first he could hardly stand for joy, the chance of speaking to another man was so delightful; but as the boat drew near there was something, he could not tell what, that was different from the boats which he had been used to all his life, and when it touched the shore he saw that the people that filled it were beings of another world than ours. Then he hastily stepped behind the wood stack, and waited for what might happen next.

The strange folk one by one jumped on to the rocks, each bearing a load of something that they wanted. Among the women he remarked two young girls, more beautiful and better dressed than any of the rest, carrying between them two great baskets full of provisions. The young man peeped out cautiously to see what all this crowd could be doing inside the tiny hut, but in a moment he drew back again, as the girls returned, and looked about as if they wanted to find out what sort of a place the island was.

Their sharp eyes soon discovered the form of a man crouching behind the bundles of sticks, and at first they felt a little frightened, and started as if they would run away. But the youth remained so still, that they took courage and laughed gaily to each other. "What a strange creature, let us try what he is made of," said one, and she stooped down and gave him a pinch.

Now the young man had a pin sticking in the sleeve of his jacket, and the moment the girl's hand touched him she pricked it so sharply that the blood came. The girl screamed so loudly that the people all ran out of their huts to see what was the matter. But directly they caught sight of the man they turned and fled in the other direction, and picking up the goods they had brought with them scampered as fast as they could down to the shore. In an instant, boat, people, and goods had vanished completely.

In their hurry they had, however, forgotten two things: a bundle of keys which lay on the table, and the girl whom the pin had pricked, and who now stood pale and helpless beside the wood stack.

"You will have to make me your wife," she said at last, "for you have drawn my blood, and I belong to you."

"Why not? I am quite willing," answered he. "But how do you suppose we can manage to live till summer comes around again?"

"Do not be anxious about that," said the girl; "if you will only marry me all will be well. I am very rich, and all my family are rich also."

Then the young man gave her his promise to make her his wife, and the girl fulfilled her part of the bargain, and food was plentiful on the island all through the long winter months, though he never knew how it got there. And by-and-by it was spring once more, and time for the fishing-folk to sail from the mainland.

"Where are we to go now?" asked the girl, one day, when the sun seemed brighter and the wind softer than usual.

"I do not care where I go," answered the young man; "what do you think?"

The girl replied that she would like to go somewhere right at the other end of the island, and build a house, far away from the huts of the fishing-folk. And he consented, and that very day they set off in search of a sheltered spot on the banks of a stream, so that it would be easy to get water.

In a tiny bay, on the opposite side of the island, they found the very thing, which seemed to have been made on purpose for them; and as they were tired with their long walk, they laid themselves down on a bank of moss among some birches and prepared to have a good night's rest, so as to be fresh for work next day. But before she went to sleep the girl turned to her husband, and said: "If in your dreams you fancy that you hear strange noises, be sure you do not stir, or get up to see what it is."

"Oh, it is not likely we shall hear any noises in such a quiet place," answered he, and fell sound asleep.

Suddenly he was awakened by a great clatter about his ears, as if all the workmen in the world were sawing and hammering and building close to him. He was just going to spring up and go to see what it meant, when he luckily remembered his wife's words and lay still. But the time till morning seemed very long, and with the first ray of sun they both rose, and pushed aside the branches of the birch trees. There, in the very place they had chosen, stood a beautiful house—doors and windows, and everything all complete!

"Now you must fix on a spot for your cow-stalls," said the girl, when they had breakfasted off wild cherries; "and take care it is the proper size, neither too large nor too small." And the husband did as he was bid, though he wondered what use a cow-house could be, as they had no cows to put in it. But as he was a little afraid of his wife, who knew so much more than he, he asked no questions.

The Elf Maiden

This night also he was awakened by the same sounds as before, and in the morning they found, near the stream, the most beautiful cow-house that ever was seen, with stalls and milk-pails and stools all complete, indeed, everything that a cow-house could possibly want, except the cows. Then the girl bade him measure out the ground for a store-house, and this, she said, might be as large as he pleased; and when the storehouse was ready she proposed that they should set off to pay her parents a visit.

The old people welcomed them heartily, and summoned their neighbors, for many miles around, to a great feast in their honor. In fact, for several weeks there was no work done on the farm at all; and at length the young man and his wife grew tired of so much play, and declared that they must return to their own home. But, before they started on the journey, the wife whispered to her husband: "Take care to jump over the threshold as quick as you can, or it will be the worse for you."

The young man listened to her words, and sprang over the threshold like an arrow from a bow; and it was well he did, for, no sooner was he on the other side, than his father-in-law threw a great hammer at him, which would have broken both his legs, if it had only touched them.

When they had gone some distance on the road home, the girl turned to her husband and said: "Till you step inside the house, be sure you do not look back, whatever you may hear or see."

And the husband promised, and for a while all was still; and he thought no more about the matter till he noticed at last that the nearer he drew to the house the louder grew the noise of the trampling of feet behind him. As he laid his hand upon the door he thought he was safe, and turned to look. There, sure enough, was a vast herd of cattle, which had been sent after him by his father-in-law when he found that his daughter had been cleverer than he. Half of the herd were already through the fence and cropping the grass on the banks of the stream, but half still remained outside and faded into nothing, even as he watched them.

However, enough cattle were left to make the young man rich, and he and his wife lived happily together, except that every now and then the girl vanished from his sight, and never told him where she had been. For a long time be kept silent about it; but one day, when he had been complaining of her absence, she said to him: "Dear husband, I am bound to go, even against my will, and there is only one way to stop me. Drive a nail into the threshold, and then I can never pass in or out."

And so he did.

Little Red Riding-hood

❦

ONCE UPON A TIME there lived in a certain village a little country girl, the prettiest creature that was ever seen. Her mother was excessively fond of her; and her grandmother doted on her still more. This good woman got made for her a little red riding-hood; which became the girl so extremely well that everybody called her Little Red Riding-hood.

One day her mother, having made some custards, said to her:

"Go, my dear, and see how thy grandmamma does, for I hear she has been very ill; carry her a custard, and this little pot of butter."

Little Red Riding-hood set out immediately to go to her grandmother, who lived in another village.

As she was going through the wood, she met with Gaffer Wolf, who had a very great mind to eat her up, but he durst not, because of some woodsmen hard by in the forest. He asked her whither she was going. The poor child, who did not know that it was dangerous to stay and hear a wolf talk, said to him:

"I am going to see my grandmamma and carry her a custard and a little pot of butter from my mamma."

"Does she live far off?" said the Wolf.

"Oh! ay," answered Little Red Riding-hood; "it is beyond that mill you see there, at the first house in the village."

"Well," said the Wolf, "and I'll go and see her too. I'll go this way and go you that, and we shall see who will be there soonest."

The Wolf began to run as fast as he could, taking the nearest way, and the little girl went by that farthest about, diverting herself in gathering nuts, running after butterflies, and making nosegays of such little flowers as she met with. The Wolf was not long before he got to the old woman's house. He knocked at the door—tap, tap.

"Who's there?"

"Your grandchild, Little Red Riding-hood," replied the Wolf, counterfeiting her voice; "who has brought you a custard and a little pot of butter sent you by mamma."

The good grandmother, who was in bed, because she was somewhat ill, cried out:

"Pull the bobbin, and the latch will go up."

The Wolf pulled the bobbin, and the door opened, and then presently he fell upon the good woman and ate her up in a moment, for it

was above three days that he had not touched a bit. He then shut the door and went into the grandmother's bed, expecting Little Red Riding-hood, who came some time afterward and knocked at the door—tap, tap.

"Who's there?"

Little Red Riding-hood, hearing the big voice of the Wolf, was first afraid; but believing her grandmother had got a cold and was hoarse, answered:

"'Tis your grandchild, Little Red Riding-hood, who has brought you a custard and a little pot of butter mamma sends you."

The Wolf cried out to her, softening his voice as much as he could:

"Pull the bobbin, and the latch will go up."

Little Red Riding-hood pulled the bobbin, and the door opened.

The Wolf, seeing her come in, said to her, hiding himself under the bedclothes:

"Put the custard and the little pot of butter upon the stool, and come and lie down with me."

Little Red Riding-hood undressed herself and went into bed, where, being greatly amazed to see how her grandmother looked in her night-clothes, she said to her:

"Grandmamma, what great arms you have got!"

"That is the better to hug thee, my dear."

"Grandmamma, what great legs you have got!"

"That is to run the better, my child."

"Grandmamma, what great ears you have got!"

"That is to hear the better, my child."

"Grandmamma, what great eyes you have got!"

"It is to see the better, my child."

"Grandmamma, what great teeth you have got!"

"That is to eat thee up."

And, saying these words, this wicked wolf fell upon Little Red Riding-hood, and ate her all up.

The Twelve
Dancing Princesses

❦

ONCE UPON A TIME there lived in the village of Montignies-sur-Roc a little cowboy, without either father or mother. His real name was Michael, but he was always called the Star Gazer, because when he drove his cows over the commons to seek for pasture, he went along with his head in the air, gaping at nothing.

As he had a fair skin, blue eyes and hair that curled all over his head, the village girls used to cry after him, "Well, Star Gazer, what are you doing?" and Michael would answer, "Oh, nothing," and go on his way without even turning to look at them.

The fact was he thought them very ugly, with their sunburned necks, their great red hands, their coarse petticoats and their wooden shoes. He had heard that somewhere in the world there were girls whose necks were pale and whose hands were small, who were always dressed in the finest silks, and were called princesses, and while his companions around the fire saw nothing in the flames but common everyday fancies, he dreamed that he had the happiness to marry a princess.

One morning about the middle of August, just at midday when the sun was hottest, Michael ate his dinner of a piece of dry bread, and went to sleep under an oak. And while he slept he dreamed that there appeared before him a beautiful lady, dressed in a robe of cloth of gold,

255

who said to him: "Go to the castle of Belœil, and there you shall marry a princess."

That evening the little cowboy, who had been thinking a great deal about the advice of the lady in the golden dress, told his dream to the farm people. But, as was natural, they only laughed at the Star Gazer.

The next day at the same hour he went to sleep again under the same tree. The lady appeared to him a second time, and said: "Go to the castle of Belœil, and you shall marry a princess."

In the evening Michael told his friends that he had dreamed the same dream again, but they only laughed at him more than before. "Never mind," he thought to himself; "if the lady appears to me a third time, I will do as she tells me."

The following day, to the great astonishment of all the village, about two o'clock in the afternoon a voice was heard singing:

> "Raleô, raleô,
> How the cattle go!"

It was the little cowboy driving his herd back to the byre.

The farmer began to scold him furiously, but he answered quietly, "I am going away," made his clothes into a bundle, said good-bye to all his friends, and boldly set out to seek his fortunes.

There was great excitement through all the village, and on the top of the hill the people stood holding their sides with laughing, as they watched the Star Gazer trudging bravely along the valley with his bundle at the end of his stick.

It was enough to make anyone laugh, certainly.

It was well known for full twenty miles around that there lived in the castle of Belœil twelve princesses of wonderful beauty, and as proud as they were beautiful, and who were besides so very sensitive and of such truly royal blood, that they would have felt at once the presence of a pea in their beds, even if the mattresses had been laid over it.

It was whispered about that they led exactly the lives that princesses ought to lead, sleeping far into the morning, and never getting up till midday. They had twelve beds all in the same room, but what was very extraordinary was the fact that though they were locked in by triple bolts, every morning their satin shoes were found worn into holes.

When they were asked what they had been doing all night, they always answered that they had been asleep; and, indeed, no noise was ever heard in the room, yet the shoes could not wear themselves out alone!

At last the Duke of Belœil ordered the trumpet to be sounded, and a proclamation to be made that whoever could discover how his daughters wore out their shoes should choose one of them for his wife.

On hearing the proclamation a number of princes arrived at the castle to try their luck. They watched all night behind the open door of the princesses, but when the morning came they had all disappeared, and no one could tell what had become of them.

When he reached the castle, Michael went straight to the gardener and offered his services. Now it happened that the garden boy had just been sent away, and though the Star Gazer did not look very sturdy, the gardener agreed to take him, as he thought that his pretty face and golden curls would please the princesses.

The first thing he was told was that when the princesses got up he was to present each one with a bouquet, and Michael thought that if he had nothing more unpleasant to do than that he should get on very well.

Accordingly he placed himself behind the door of the princesses' room, with the twelve bouquets in a basket. He gave one to each of the sisters, and they took them without even deigning to look at the lad, except Lina the youngest, who fixed her large black eyes as soft as velvet on him, and exclaimed, "Oh, how pretty he is—our new flower boy!" The rest all burst out laughing, and the eldest pointed out that a princess ought never to lower herself by looking at a garden boy.

Now Michael knew quite well what had happened to all the princes, but notwithstanding, the beautiful eyes of the Princess Lina inspired him with a violent longing to try his fate. Unhappily he did not dare to come forward, being afraid that he should only be jeered at, or even turned away from the castle on account of his impudence.

Nevertheless, the Star Gazer had another dream. The lady in the golden dress appeared to him once more, holding in one hand two young laurel trees, a cherry laurel and a rose laurel, and in the other hand a little golden rake, a little golden bucket, and a silken towel. She thus addressed him:

"Plant these two laurels in two large pots, rake them over with the rake, water them with the bucket, and wipe them with the towel. When they have grown as tall as a girl of fifteen, say to each of them, 'My beautiful laurel, with the golden rake I have raked you, with the golden bucket I have watered you, with the silken towel I have wiped you.' Then after that ask anything you choose, and the laurels will give it to you."

Michael thanked the lady in the golden dress, and when he woke he found the two laurel bushes beside him. So he carefully obeyed the orders he had been given by the lady.

The trees grew very fast, and when they were as tall as a girl of fifteen he said to the cherry laurel, "My lovely cherry laurel, with the golden rake I have raked thee, with the golden bucket I have watered thee, with the silken towel I have wiped thee. Teach me how to become invisible." Then there instantly appeared on the laurel a pretty white flower, which Michael gathered and stitched into his buttonhole.

That evening, when the princesses went upstairs to bed, he followed them barefoot, so that he might make no noise, and hid himself under one of the twelve beds, so as not to take up much room.

The princesses began at once to open their wardrobes and boxes. They took out of them the most magnificent dresses, which they put on before their mirrors, and when they had finished, turned themselves all around to admire their appearances.

Michael could see nothing from his hidingplace, but he could hear everything, and he listened to the princesses laughing and jumping with pleasure. At last the eldest said, "Be quick, my sisters, our partners will be impatient." At the end of an hour, when the Star Gazer heard no more noise, he peeped out and saw the twelve sisters in splendid garments, with their satin shoes on their feet, and in their hands the bouquets he had brought them.

"Are you ready?" asked the eldest.

"Yes," replied the other eleven in chorus, and they took their places one by one behind her.

Then the eldest Princess clapped her hands three times and a trap door opened. All the princesses disappeared down a secret staircase, and Michael hastily followed them.

As he was following on the steps of the Princess Lina, he carelessly trod on her dress.

"There is somebody behind me," cried the Princess; "they are holding my dress."

"You foolish thing," said her eldest sister, "you are always afraid of something. It is only a nail which caught you."

The Twelve Dancing Princesses

They went down, down, down, till at last they came to a passage with a door at one end, which was only fastened with a latch. The eldest Princess opened it, and they found themselves immediately in a lovely little wood, where the leaves were spangled with drops of silver which shone in the brilliant light of the moon.

They next crossed another wood where the leaves were sprinkled with gold, and after that another still, where the leaves glittered with diamonds.

At last the Star Gazer perceived a large lake, and on the shores of the lake twelve little boats with awnings, in which were seated twelve princes, who, grasping their oars, awaited the princesses.

Each princess entered one of the boats, and Michael slipped into that which held the youngest. The boats glided along rapidly, but Lina's, from being heavier, was always behind the rest. "We never went so slowly before," said the Princess; "what can be the reason?"

"I don't know," answered the Prince. "I assure you I am rowing as hard as I can."

On the other side of the lake the garden boy saw a beautiful castle splendidly illuminated, whence came the lively music of fiddles, kettledrums, and trumpets.

In a moment they touched land, and the company jumped out of the boats; and the princes, after having securely fastened their barques, gave their arms to the princesses and conducted them to the castle.

Michael followed, and entered the ballroom in their train. Everywhere were mirrors, lights, flowers, and damask hangings.

The Star Gazer was quite bewildered at the magnificence of the sight.

He placed himself out of the way in a corner, admiring the grace and beauty of the princesses. Their loveliness was of every kind. Some were fair and some were dark; some had chestnut hair, or curls darker still, and some had golden locks. Never were so many beautiful princesses seen together at one time, but the one whom the cowboy thought the most beautiful and the most fascinating was the little Princess with the velvet eyes.

With what eagerness she danced! leaning on her partner's shoulder she swept by like a whirlwind. Her cheeks flushed, her eyes sparkled, and it was plain that she loved dancing better than anything else.

The poor boy envied those handsome young men with whom she danced so gracefully, but he did not know how little reason he had to be jealous of them.

The young men were really the princes who, to the number of fifty at least, had tried to steal the princesses' secret. The princesses had made them drink something of a philter, which froze the heart and left nothing but the love of dancing.

They danced on till the shoes of the princesses were worn into holes. When the cock crowed the third time the fiddles stopped, and a delicious supper was served by boys, consisting of sugared orange flowers, crystallized rose leaves, powdered violets, cracknels, wafers, and other dishes, which are, as everyone knows, the favorite food of princesses.

After supper, the dancers all went back to their boats, and this time the Star Gazer entered that of the eldest Princess. They crossed again the wood with the diamond-spangled leaves, the wood with gold-sprinkled leaves, and the wood whose leaves glittered with drops of silver, and as a proof of what he had seen, the boy broke a small branch from a tree in the last wood. Lina turned as she heard the noise made by the breaking of the branch.

"What was that noise?" she said.

"It was nothing," replied her eldest sister; "it was only the screech of the barn-owl that roosts in one of the turrets of the castle."

While she was speaking Michael managed to slip in front, and running up the staircase, he reached the princesses' room first. He flung open the window, and sliding down the vine which climbed up the wall, found himself in the garden just as the sun was beginning to rise, and it was time for him to set to his work.

That day, when he made up the bouquets, Michael hid the branch with the silver drops in the nosegay intended for the youngest Princess.

When Lina discovered it she was much surprised. However, she said nothing to her sisters, but as she met the boy by accident while she was walking under the shade of the elms, she suddenly stopped as if to speak to him; then, altering her mind, went on her way.

The same evening the twelve sisters went again to the ball, and the Star Gazer again followed them and crossed the lake in Lina's boat.

This time it was the Prince who complained that the boat seemed very heavy.

"It is the heat," replied the Princess. "I, too, have been feeling very warm."

During the ball she looked everywhere for the gardener's boy, but she never saw him.

As they came back, Michael gathered a branch from the wood with the gold-spangled leaves, and now it was the eldest Princess who heard the noise that it made in breaking.

"It is nothing," said Lina; "only the cry of the owl which roosts in the turrets of the castle."

As soon as she got up she found the branch in her bouquet. When the sisters went down she stayed a little behind and said to the cowboy: "Where does this branch come from?"

"Your Royal Highness knows well enough," answered Michael.

"So you have followed us?"

"Yes, Princess."

"How did you manage it? We never saw you."

"I hid myself," replied the Star Gazer quietly.

The Princess was silent a moment, and then said:

"You know our secret!—keep it. Here is the reward of your discretion." And she flung the boy a purse of gold.

"I do not sell my silence," answered Michael, and he went away without picking up the purse.

For three nights Lina neither saw nor heard anything extraordinary; on the fourth she heard a rustling among the diamond-spangled leaves of the wood. That day there was a branch of the trees in her bouquet.

She took the Star Gazer aside, and said to him in a harsh voice:

"You know what price my father has promised to pay for our secret?"

"I know, Princess," answered Michael.

"Don't you mean to tell him?"

"That is not my intention."

"Are you afraid?"

"No, Princess."

"What makes you so discreet, then?"

But Michael was silent.

Lina's sisters had seen her talking to the little garden boy, and jeered at her for it.

"What prevents your marrying him?" asked the eldest. "You would become a gardener too; it is a charming profession. You could live in a cottage at the end of the park, and help your husband to draw up water from the well, and when we get up you could bring us our bouquets."

The Princess Lina was very angry, and when the Star Gazer presented her bouquet, she received it in a disdainful manner.

Michael behaved most respectfully. He never raised his eyes to her, but nearly all day she felt him at her side without ever seeing him.

One day she made up her mind to tell everything to her eldest sister.

"What!" said she, "this rogue knows our secret, and you never told me! I must lose no time in getting rid of him."

"But how?"

"Why, by having him taken to the tower with the dungeons, of course."

For this was the way that in old times beautiful princesses got rid of people who knew too much.

But the astonishing part of it was that the youngest sister did not seem at all to relish this method of stopping the mouth of the gardener's boy, who, after all, had said nothing to their father.

It was agreed that the question should be submitted to the other ten sisters. All were on the side of the eldest. Then the youngest sister declared that if they laid a finger on the little garden boy, she would herself go and tell their father the secret of the holes in their shoes.

At last it was decided that Michael should be put to the test; that they would take him to the ball, and at the end of supper would give him the philter which was to enchant him like the rest.

They sent for the Star Gazer, and asked him how he had contrived to learn their secret; but still he remained silent.

Then, in commanding tones, the eldest sister gave him the order they had agreed upon.

He only answered:

"I will obey."

He had really been present, invisible, at the council of princesses, and had heard all; but he had make up his mind to drink of the philter, and sacrifice himself to the happiness of her he loved.

Not wishing, however, to cut a poor figure at the ball by the side of the other dancers, he went at once to the laurels, and said:

"My lovely rose laurel, with the golden rake I have raked thee, with the golden bucket I have watered thee, with a silken towel I have dried thee. Dress me like a prince."

A beautiful pink flower appeared. Michael gathered it, and found himself in a moment clothed in velvet, which was as black as the eyes of the little Princess, with a cap to match, a diamond aigrette, and a blossom of the rose laurel in his buttonhole.

Thus dressed, he presented himself that evening before the Duke of Belœil, and obtained leave to try and discover his daughters' secret. He looked so distinguished that hardly anyone would have known who he was.

The twelve princesses went upstairs to bed. Michael followed them, and waited behind the open door till they gave the signal for departure.

This time he did not cross in Lina's boat. He gave his arm to the eldest sister, danced with each in turn, and was so graceful that everyone was delighted with him. At last the time came for him to dance with the little Princess. She found him the best partner in the world, but he did not dare to speak a single word to her.

When he was taking her back to her place she said to him in a mocking voice:

"Here you are at the summit of your wishes: you are being treated like a prince."

"Don't be afraid," replied the Star Gazer gently. "You shall never be a gardener's wife."

The little Princess stared at him with a frightened face, and he left her without waiting for an answer.

When the satin slippers were worn through the fiddles stopped, and the serving boys set the table. Michael was placed next to the eldest sister, and opposite to the youngest.

They gave him the most exquisite dishes to eat, and the most delicate wines to drink; and in order to turn his head more completely, compliments and flattery were heaped on him from every side.

But he took care not to be intoxicated, either by the wine or the compliments.

❦　❦　❦

The Twelve Dancing Princesses

At last the eldest sister made a sign, and one of the pages brought in a large golden cup.

"The enchanted castle has no more secrets for you," she said to the Star Gazer. "Let us drink to your triumph."

He cast a lingering glance at the little Princess, and without hesitation lifted the cup.

"Don't drink!" suddenly cried out the little Princess; "I would rather marry a gardener."

And she burst into tears.

Michael flung the contents of the cup behind him, sprang over the table, and fell at Lina's feet. The rest of the princes fell likewise at the knees of the princesses, each of whom chose a husband and raised him to her side. The charm was broken.

The twelve couples embarked in the boats, which crossed back many times in order to carry over the other princes. Then they all went through the three woods, and when they had passed the door of the underground passage a great noise was heard, as if the enchanted castle was crumbling to the earth.

They went straight to the room of the Duke of Belœil, who had just awoke. Michael held in his hand the golden cup, and he revealed the secret of the holes in the shoes.

"Choose, then," said the Duke, "whichever you prefer."

"My choice is already made," replied the garden boy, and he offered his hand to the youngest Princess, who blushed and lowered her eyes.

The Princess Lina did not become a gardener's wife; on the contrary, it was the Star Gazer who became a Prince: but before the marriage ceremony the Princess insisted that her lover should tell her how he came to discover the secret.

The Twelve Dancing Princesses

So he showed her the two laurels which had helped him, and she, like a prudent girl, thinking they gave him too much advantage over his wife, cut them off at the root and threw them in the fire. And this is why the country girls go about singing:

> "*Nous n'irons plus au bois,*
> *Les lauriers sont coupés,*"

and dancing in summer by the light of the moon.

The Crab and the Monkey

THERE WAS ONCE a crab who lived in a hole on the shady side of a mountain. She was a very good housewife, and so careful and industrious that there was no creature in the whole country whose hole was so neat and clean as hers, and she took great pride in it.

One day she saw lying near the mouth of her hole a handful of cooked rice which some pilgrim must have let fall when he was stopping to eat his dinner. Delighted at this discovery, she hastened to the spot, and was carrying the rice back to her hole when a monkey, who lived in some trees nearby, came down to see what the crab was doing. His eyes shone at the sight of the rice, for it was his favorite food, and like the sly fellow he was, he proposed a bargain to the crab. She was to give him half the rice in exchange for the kernel of a sweet red kaki fruit which he had just eaten. He half expected that the crab would laugh in his face at this impudent proposal, but instead of doing so she only looked at him for a moment with her head on one side and then said that she would agree to the exchange. So the monkey went off with his rice, and the crab returned to her hole with the kernel.

For some time the crab saw no more of the monkey, who had gone to pay a visit on the sunny side of the mountain; but one morning he happened to pass by her hole, and found her sitting under the shadow of a beautiful kaki tree.

The Crab and the Monkey

"Good day," he said politely, "you have some very fine fruit there! I am very hungry, could you spare me one or two?"

"Oh, certainly," replied the crab, "but you must forgive me if I cannot get them for you myself. I am no tree-climber."

"Pray do not apologize," answered the monkey. "Now that I have your permission I can get them myself quite easily." And the crab consented to let him go up, merely saying that he must throw her down half the fruit.

In another moment he was swinging himself from branch to branch, eating all the ripest kakis and filling his pockets with the rest, and the poor crab saw to her disgust that the few he threw down to her were either not ripe at all or else quite rotten.

"You are a shocking rogue," she called in a rage; but the monkey took no notice, and went on eating as fast as he could. The crab understood that it was no use her scolding, so she resolved to try what cunning would do.

"Sir Monkey," she said, "you are certainly a very good climber, but now that you have eaten so much, I am quite sure you would never be able to turn one of your somersaults."

The monkey prided himself on turning better somersaults than any of his family, so he instantly went head over heels three times on the bough on which he was sitting, and all the beautiful kakis that he had in his pockets rolled to the ground. Quick as lightning the crab picked them up and carried a quantity of them into her house, but when she came up for another the monkey sprang on her, and treated her so badly that he left her for dead. When he had beaten her till his arm ached he went his way.

It was a lucky thing for the poor crab that she had some friends to come to her help or she certainly would have died then and there. The

wasp flew to her, and took her back to bed and looked after her, and then he consulted with a rice-mortar and an egg which had fallen out of a nest nearby, and they agreed that when the monkey returned, as he was sure to do, to steal the rest of the fruit, that they would punish him severely for the manner in which he had behaved to the crab. So the mortar climbed up to the beam over the front door, and the egg lay quite still on the ground, while the wasp set down the water-bucket in a corner. Then the crab dug itself a deep hole in the ground, so that not even the tip of her claws might be seen.

Soon after everything was ready the monkey jumped down from his tree, and creeping to the door began a long hypocritical speech, asking pardon for all he had done. He waited for an answer of some sort, but none came. He listened, but all was still; then he peeped, and saw no one; then he went in. He peered about for the crab, but in vain; however, his eyes fell on the egg, which he snatched up and set on the fire. But in a moment the egg had burst into a thousand pieces, and its sharp shell struck him in the face and scratched him horribly. Smarting with pain he ran to the bucket and stooped down to throw some water over his head. As he stretched out his hand up started the wasp and stung him on the nose. The monkey shrieked and ran to the door, but as he passed through down fell the mortar and struck him dead. After that the crab lived happily for many years, and at length died in peace under her own kaki tree.

The Six Swans

❦

A KING WAS ONCE HUNTING in a great wood, and he hunted the game so eagerly that none of his courtiers could follow him. When evening came on he stood still and looked around him, and he saw that he had quite lost himself. He sought a way out, but could find none. Then he saw an old woman with a shaking head coming toward him; but she was a witch.

"Good woman," he said to her, "can you not show me the way out of the wood?"

"Oh, certainly, Sir King," she replied, "I can quite well do that, but on one condition, which if you do not fulfill you will never get out of the wood, and will die of hunger."

"What is the condition?" asked the King.

"I have a daughter," said the old woman, "who is so beautiful that she has not her equal in the world, and is well fitted to be your wife; if you will make her lady-queen I will show you the way out of the wood."

The King in his anguish of mind consented, and the old woman led him to her little house where her daughter was sitting by the fire. She received the King as if she were expecting him, and he saw that she was certainly very beautiful; but she did not please him, and he could not look at her without a secret feeling of horror. As soon as he had lifted the maiden on to his horse the old woman showed him the way, and

the King reached his palace, where the wedding was celebrated.

The King had already been married once, and had by his first wife seven children, six boys and one girl, whom he loved more than anything in the world. And now, because he was afraid that their stepmother might not treat them well and might do them harm, he put them in a lonely castle that stood in the middle of a wood. It lay so hidden, and the way to it was so hard to find, that he himself could not have found it out had not a wise-woman given him a reel of thread which possessed a marvelous property: when he threw it before him it unwound itself and showed him the way. But the King went so often to his dear children that the Queen was offended at his absence. She grew curious, and wanted to know what he had to do quite alone in the wood. She gave his servants a great deal of money, and they betrayed the secret to her, and also told her of the reel which alone could point out the way. She had no rest now till she had found out where the King guarded the reel, and then she made some little white shirts, and, as she had learned from her witch-mother, sewed an enchantment in each of them.

And when the King had ridden off she took the little shirts and went into the wood, and the reel showed her the way. The children, who saw someone coming in the distance, thought it was their dear father coming to them, and sprang to meet him very joyfully. Then she threw over each one a little shirt, which when it had touched their bodies changed them into swans, and they flew away over the forest. The Queen went home quite satisfied, and thought she had got rid of her stepchildren; but the girl had not run to meet her with her brothers, and she knew nothing of her.

The next day the King came to visit his children, but he found no one but the girl.

"Where are your brothers?" asked the King.

"Alas! dear father," she answered, "they have gone away and left me all alone." And she told him that looking out of her little window she had seen her brothers flying over the wood in the shape of swans, and she showed him the feathers which they had let fall in the yard, and which she had collected. The King mourned, but he did not think that the Queen had done the wicked deed, and as he was afraid the maiden would also be taken from him, he wanted to take her with him. But she was afraid of the stepmother, and begged the King to let her stay just one night more in the castle in the wood. The poor maiden thought, "My home is no longer here; I will go and seek my brothers." And when night came she fled away into the forest. She ran all through the night and the next day, till she could go no farther for weariness. Then she saw a little hut, went in, and found a room with six little beds. She was afraid to lie down on one, so she crept under one of them, lay on the hard floor, and was going to spend the night there. But when the sun had set she heard a noise, and saw six swans flying in at the window. They stood on the floor and blew at one another, and blew all their feathers off, and their swan-skin came off like a shirt. Then the maiden recognized her brothers, and overjoyed she crept out from under the bed. Her brothers were not less delighted than she to see their little sister again, but their joy did not last long.

"You cannot stay here," they said to her. "This is a den of robbers; if they were to come here and find you they would kill you."

"Could you not protect me?" asked the little sister.

"No," they answered, "for we can only lay aside our swan-skins for a quarter of an hour every evening. For this time we regain our human forms, but then we are changed into swans again."

Then the little sister cried and said, "Can you not be freed?"

"Oh, no," they said, "the conditions are too hard. You must not speak or laugh for six years, and must make in that time six shirts for us out of star-flowers. If a single word comes out of your mouth, all your labor is vain." And when the brothers had said this the quarter of an hour came to an end, and they flew away out of the window as swans.

But the maiden had determined to free her brothers even if it should cost her her life. She left the hut, went into the forest, climbed a tree, and spent the night there. The next morning she went out, collected star-flowers, and began to sew. She could speak to no one, and she had no wish to laugh, so she sat there, looking only at her work.

When she had lived there some time, it happened that the King of the country was hunting in the forest, and his hunters came to the tree on which the maiden sat. They called to her and said, "Who are you?"

But she gave no answer.

"Come down to us," they said, "we will do you no harm."

But she shook her head silently. As they pressed her further with questions, she threw them the golden chain from her neck. But they did not leave off, and she threw them her girdle, and when this was no use, her garters, and then her dress. The huntsmen would not leave her alone, but climbed the tree, lifted the maiden down, and led her to the King. The King asked, "Who are you? What are you doing up that tree?"

But she answered nothing.

He asked her in all the languages he knew, but she remained as dumb as a fish. Because she was so beautiful, however, the King's heart was touched, and he was seized with a great love for her. He wrapped her up in his cloak, placed her before him on his horse, and brought her to his castle. There he had her dressed in rich clothes, and her beauty shone out as bright as day, but not a word could be drawn from her. He set her at table by his side, and her modest ways and behavior pleased him so much that he said, "I will marry this maiden and none other in the world," and after some days he married her. But the King had a wicked mother who was displeased with the marriage, and said wicked things of the young Queen. "Who knows who this girl is?" she said; "she cannot speak, and is not worthy of a king."

After a year, when the Queen had her first child, the old mother took it away from her. Then she went to the King and said that the Queen had killed it. The King would not believe it, and would not allow any harm to be done her. But she sat quietly sewing at the shirts and troubling herself about nothing. The next time she had a child the wicked mother did the same thing, but the King could not make up his mind to believe her. He said, "She is too sweet and good to do such a thing as that. If she were not dumb and could defend herself, her innocence would be proved." But when the third child was taken away,

and the Queen was again accused, and could not utter a word in her own defense, the King was obliged to give her over to the law, which decreed that she must be burned to death. When the day came on which the sentence was to be executed, it was the last day of the six years in which she must not speak or laugh, and now she had freed her dear brothers from the power of the enchantment. The six shirts were done; there was only the left sleeve wanting to the last.

When she was led to the stake, she laid the shirts on her arm, and as she stood on the pile and the fire was about to be lighted, she looked around her and saw six swans flying through the air. Then she knew that her release was at hand and her heart danced for joy. The swans fluttered around her, and hovered low so that she could throw the shirts over them. When they had touched them the swan-skins fell off, and her brothers stood before her living, well and beautiful. Only the youngest had a swan's wing instead of his left arm. They embraced and kissed each other, and the Queen went to the King, who was standing by in great astonishment, and began to speak to him, saying, "Dearest husband, now I can speak and tell you openly that I am innocent and have been falsely accused."

She told him of the old woman's deceit, and how she had taken the three children away and hidden them. Then they were fetched, to the great joy of the King, and the wicked mother came to no good end.

But the King and the Queen with their six brothers lived many years in happiness and peace.

The Street Musicians

A MAN ONCE POSSESSED a donkey which had served him faithfully for many years, but at last the poor beast grew old and feeble, and every day his work became more of a burden. As he was no longer of any use, his master made up his mind to shoot him; but when the donkey learned the fate that was in store for him, he determined not to die, but to run away to the nearest town and there to become a street musician.

When he had trotted along for some distance he came upon a greyhound lying on the road, and panting for dear life. "Well, brother," said the donkey, "what's the matter with you? You look rather tired."

"So I am," replied the dog, "but because I am getting old and am growing weaker every day, and cannot go out hunting any longer, my master wanted to poison me; and, as life is still sweet, I have taken leave of him. But how I am to earn my own livelihood I haven't a notion."

"Well," said the donkey, "I am on my way to the nearest big town, where I mean to become a street musician. Why don't you take up music as a profession and come along with me? I'll play the flute and you can play the kettle-drum."

The greyhound was quite pleased at the idea, and the two set off together. When they had gone a short distance they met a cat with a face as long as three rainy days. "Now, what has happened to upset your happiness, friend puss?" inquired the donkey.

"It's impossible to look cheerful when one feels depressed," answered the cat. "I am well up in years now, and have lost most of my teeth; consequently I prefer sitting in front of the fire to catching mice, and so my old mistress wanted to drown me. I have no wish to die yet, so I ran away from her; but good advice is expensive, and I don't know where I am to go to, or what I am to do."

"Come to the nearest big town with us," said the donkey, "and try your fortune as a street musician. I know what sweet music you make at night, so you are sure to be a success."

The cat was delighted with the donkey's proposal, and they all continued their journey together. In a short time they came to the courtyard of an inn, where they found a cock crowing lustily. "What in the world is the matter with you?" asked the donkey. "The noise you are making is enough to break the drums of our ears."

"I am only prophesying good weather," said the cock; "for tomorrow is a feast day, and just because it is a holiday and a number of people are expected at the inn, the landlady has given orders for my neck to be wrung tonight, so that I may be made into soup for tomorrow's dinner."

"I'll tell you what, redcap," said the donkey; "you had much better come with us to the nearest town. You have got a good voice, and could join a street band we are getting up." The cock was much pleased with the idea, and the party proceeded on their way.

But the nearest big town was a long way off, and it took them more than a day to reach it. In the evening they came to a wood, and they made up their minds to go no farther, but to spend the night there. The donkey and the greyhound lay down under a big tree, and the cat and the cock got up into the branches, the cock flying right up to the topmost twig, where he thought he would be safe from all danger. Before he went to sleep he looked around the four points of the compass, and saw a little spark burning in the distance. He called out to his companions that he was sure there must be a house not far off, for he could see a light shining.

When he heard this, the donkey said at once: "Then we must get up, and go and look for the house, for this is very poor shelter." And the greyhound added: "Yes; I feel I'd be all the better for a few bones and a scrap or two of meat."

So they set out for the spot where the light was to be seen shining faintly in the distance, but the nearer they approached it the brighter it grew, till at last they came to a brilliantly lighted house. The donkey being the biggest of the party went to the window and looked in.

"Well, greyhead, what do you see?" asked the cock.

"I see a well-covered table," replied the donkey, "with excellent food and drink, and several robbers are sitting around it, enjoying themselves highly."

"I wish we were doing the same," said the cock.

"So do I," answered the donkey. "Can't we think of some plan for turning out the robbers, and taking possession of the house ourselves?"

So they consulted together what they were to do, and at last they arranged that the donkey should stand at the window with his fore-feet on the sill, that the greyhound should get on his back, the cat on the dog's shoulder, and the cock on the cat's head. When they had grouped themselves in this way, at a given signal, they all began their different forms of music. The donkey brayed, the greyhound barked, the cat miawed, and the cock crew. Then they all scrambled through the window into the room, breaking the glass into a thousand pieces as they did so.

The robbers were all startled by the dreadful noise, and thinking that some evil spirits at the least were entering the house, they rushed out into the wood, their hair standing on end with terror. The four companions, delighted with the success of their trick, sat down at the table, and ate and drank all the food and wine that the robbers had left behind them.

When they had finished their meal they put out the lights, and each animal chose a suitable sleeping-place. The donkey lay down in the courtyard outside the house, the dog behind the door, the cat in front of the fire, and the cock flew up on to a high shelf, and, as they were all tired after their long day, they soon went to sleep.

Shortly after midnight, when the robbers saw that no light was burning in the house and that all seemed quiet, the captain of the band said: "We were fools to let ourselves be so easily frightened away"; and, turning to one of his men, he ordered him to go and see if all was safe.

The man found everything in silence and darkness, and going into the kitchen he thought he had better strike a light. He took a match, and mistaking the fiery eyes of the cat for two glowing coals, he tried to light his match with them. But the cat didn't see the joke, and sprang at his face, spitting and scratching him in the most vigorous manner. The man was terrified out of his life, and tried to run out by the back door; but he stumbled over the greyhound, which bit him in the leg. Yelling with pain he ran across the courtyard only to receive a kick from the donkey's hind leg as he passed him. In the meantime the cock had been roused from his slumbers, and feeling very cheerful he called out, from the shelf where he was perched, "Kikeriki!"

Then the robber hastened back to his captain and said: "Sir, there is a dreadful witch in the house, who spat at me and scratched my face with her long fingers; and before the door there stands a man with a long knife, who cut my leg severely. In the courtyard outside lies a vile monster, who fell upon me with a huge wooden club; and that is not all, for, sitting on the roof, is a judge, who called out: 'Bring the rascal to me.' So I fled for dear life."

The Street Musicians

After this the robbers dared not venture into the house again, and they abandoned it for ever. But the four street musicians were so delighted with their lodgings that they determined to take up their abode in the robbers' house, and, for all I know to the contrary, they may be living there to this day.

Bibliography

ANDREW LANG collected and published his twelve fairy-tale collections from 1889 through 1914. Our stories come from *The Blue Fairy Book* (1889); *The Red Fairy Book* (1890); *The Green Fairy Book* (1892); *The Yellow Fairy Book* (1894); *The Pink Fairy Book* (1897); *The Grey Fairy Book* (1900); *The Crimson Fairy Book* (1903); *The Brown Fairy Book* (1904); *The Orange Fairy Book* (1906); and *The Olive Fairy Book* (1907). We are indebted to Brian Alderson's extensive notes in the Viking/Kestrel editions of the Blue, Red, Green, Yellow and Pink books for the background information on most of these stories. For the rest, we have relied on Lang's own notes and introductions.

"Cinderella, or The Little Glass Slipper" by Charles Perrault, translated from the French. First published as "Cendrillon ou: la Petite Pantoufle de Verre" in *Histoires, ou Countes du Temps Passé* (Paris, 1697).

"The Crab and the Monkey" by David Brauns, translated from the Japanese. Published in *Japanische Märchen und Sagen* (Leipzig, 1875).

"The Cunning Hare" by the Smithsonian Bureau of Ethnology. Published in *Indian Folk Tales*.

"East of the Sun & West of the Moon" by P. C. Asbjörnsen and J. Moe, translated from the Norwegian. First published as "Østenfor Sol og Vestenfor Maane" in *Norske Folke Eventyr* (Christiania, 1842).

"The Elf Maiden," translated from the German. Published in *Lapplandische Märchen*.

Bibliography

"Father Grumbler," translated from the French. Published in *Contes Populaires*.

"The Fisherman and His Wife" by the Brothers Grimm, translated from the German. First published as "Von dem Fischer un syner Fru" in *Kinder- und Hausmärchen* (Berlin, 1812).

"The Flying Ship" by A. N. Afanasiev, translated from the Russian. First published as "Letuchi korabl" in *Skazki* (Moscow, 1855).

"Hansel and Grettel" by the Brothers Grimm, translated from the German. First published as "Hänsel und Gretel" in *Kinder- und Hausmärchen* (Berlin, 1812).

"The Hero Makóma," translated from the Rhodesian.

"The History of Jack the Giant Killer" by Edwin Sidney Hartland. First published in *English Fairy and Other Folk Tales* (London, 1890).

"Hok Lee and the Dwarfs," translated from the Chinese.

"Jack and the Beanstalk" by Joseph Jacobs. First published in *English Fairy Tales* (London, 1890).

"Little Red Riding-hood" by Charles Perrault, translated from the French. First published as "Le Petit Chaperon Rouge" in *Histoires, ou Countes du Temps Passé* (Paris, 1697).

"The Master Cat, or Puss in Boots" by Charles Perrault, translated from the French. First published as "Le Maistre Chat, ou le Chat Botté" in *Histoires, ou Countes du Temps Passé* (Paris, 1697).

"The Nightingale" by Hans Christian Andersen, translated from the Danish. First published as "Nattergalen" in *Nye Eventyr* (Copenhagen, 1843).

"The Nixy" by Dr. Herman Kletke, translated from the German. First published as "Die Nixe" in *Zeitschrift für deutsches Alterhum* (Leipzig, 1841).

"Rapunzel" by the Brothers Grimm, translated from the German. First published in *Kinder- und Hausmärchen* (Berlin, 1812).

"The Ratcatcher" by M. Charles Marelle, translated from the French.

"Rumpelstiltzkin" by the Brothers Grimm, translated from the German. First published as "Rumpelstiltzschen" in *Kinder- und Hausmärchen* (Berlin, 1812).

Bibliography

"The Six Swans" by the Brothers Grimm, translated from the German. First published as "Die Sechs Schwane" in *Kinder- und Hausmärchen* (Berlin, 1812).

"The Snake Prince," translated from the Indian by Major Campbell.

"Snow-white and Rose-red" by the Brothers Grimm, translated from the German. First published as "Schneeweisschen und Rosenrot" in *Kinder- und Hausmärchen* (Berlin, 1812).

"Snowdrop" by the Brothers Grimm, translated from the German. First published as "Sneewittchen" in *Kinder- und Hausmärchen* (Berlin, 1812).

"The Steadfast Tin Soldier" by Hans Christian Andersen, translated from the Danish. First published as "Den Standhaftige Tinsoldat" in *Eventyr* (Copenhagen, 1838).

"The Street Musicians" by Dr. Herman Kletke, translated from the German. Published in *Märchensaal: Märchen aller Völker für Jung und Alt* (Berlin, 1845).

"The Swineherd" by Hans Christian Andersen, translated from the Danish. First published as "Svinedrengen" in *Eventyr* (Copenhagen, 1842).

"The Three Little Pigs" by James Orchard Halliwell. First published in *The Nursery Rhymes of England* (London, 1853).

"The Tinderbox" by Hans Christian Andersen, translated from the Danish. First published as "Fyrtøiet" in *Eventyr* (Copenhagen, 1835).

"The Twelve Dancing Princesses" by the Brothers Grimm, translated from the German. First published as "Die Zertanzren Schuhe" in *Kinder- und Hausmärchen* (Berlin, 1812).

"The Water of Life" by D. Francisco de S. Maspons y Labros, translated from the Spanish. First published as "L'Aygua de la Vida" in *Cuentos Populars Catalans* (Barcelona, 1885).